EVACUATION PLAN

a novel from the hospice

Kathy,

Enjoy the journey.

Joe O'Connell

8/12/08

Brenham

Kathy,

Enjoy the journey.

Joe O'Connell.

8/12/08

Brenham

EVACUATION PLAN

a novel from the hospice

by

Joe M. O'Connell

Foreword by Joe Holley

Dalton Publishing
P.O. Box 242
Austin, Texas 78767
daltonpublishing.com

Copyright 2007 by Joe M. O'Connell. All rights reserved.

Printed in the United States of America.

Portions of this book were previously published in a slightly different form in *The G.W. Review* as "Marina Dreams," *Other Voices* as "Crazy Baby to Win," *Lullwater Review* as "Stardust," *New Texas* as "Walking on the Moon," *Confrontation* as "Clown Food," *Apocalypse* as "Reruns," and *Lynx Eye* as "Hangover."

Edited by Ric Williams

Cover Design by Jason Hranicky
Cover Photograph by Brian Hollingsworth

ISBN-10: 0-9740703-8-6
ISBN-13: 978-0-9740703-8-4

O'Connell, Joe M., 1959-
Evacuation plan : a novel from the hospice / by Joe M. O'Connell ; foreword by Joe Holley.
p. cm.
ISBN-13: 978-0-9740703-8-4
ISBN-10: 0-9740703-8-6
1. Hospice care--Fiction. 2. Screenwriters--Fiction. I. Title.
PS3615.C655E93 2007
813'.6--dc22

2007018322

This is a work of fiction. The characters and events in this book are fictitious. Any similarity to real persons, living or dead, is coincidental and not intended by the author.

ACKNOWLEDGMENTS

The people who inspired and guided this book's long journey to completion are many, and I hope any I leave out will forgive me. In 2001 I was chosen by *Borderlands: Texas Poetry Review* and Benné Rockett's arts organization Opening Closed Doors to join a group of fantastically talented visual artists and writers at Hospice Austin's Christopher House. I am indebted to them as well as to everyone I met at Christopher House; in particular I want to thank volunteer coordinator Wendy Bixby and the recently retired Mary Stephenson whose comment about this book's potential to make a small difference has stayed with me.

Much of this book was completed during a residency at IDEA in Austin, Texas, where I again worked with Benné Rockett and two visual artists. I am extremely grateful for the time, space, and swirling creativity. Benné, you rock.

Some of the individual stories included in this novel date back to my days in the MFA program at Southwest Texas State University. Thanks to all of my fellow students and to my writing teachers: John Blair, Debra Monroe, Miles Wilson, Tom Grimes, and Karen Brennan. The late Andre Dubus also worked long distance with me, and proved as generous a teacher as he was masterful with the written word. In addition to him, I must thank the fine writers whose works have particularly inspired me over the years: Charles Baxter (go buy a book by him immediately), Flannery O'Connor, John Irving, Tim O'Brien, Gabriel Garcia Marquez, Rick DeMarinis, Bobbie Ann Mason, Milan Kundera, Raymond Carver, and John Updike.

I'm also thankful for my teaching colleagues at Austin Community College (particularly the fine folks in the Rio Grande Campus Learning Lab) and St. Edward's University, plus the many students who have enriched my life. Film plays a role in this story, and I owe a lot to the film writing crews at *The Austin Chronicle*, *Dallas Morning News*, *Austin American-Statesman*, and *San Antonio Express-News* for welcoming me into their fold. Big thanks to Deltina Hay of Dalton Publishing for taking this book on, and to my editor Ric Williams for his keen eye and apt suggestions. Kudos to Mary Reilly for her proofreading help and to Gary Kent for being my pal/sounding board.

Last, but certainly not least, I thank my family who will recognize the tiny squares of *reality* in this patchwork quilt of fiction that really began when I started telling them my childhood tales of traveling to Mars at night. My late father's presence runs through this book (though he was a much nicer guy than Matt's dad), and I thank him and my mother for showing me the good that flows throughout this world. Of course, none of this would be possible without the constant support of my beautiful, funny, amazingly smart, and insightful wife Tiffany. Thanks for believing in me. To my newborn son Nicholas: it's about time you got here!

FOREWORD

> "For we do not, after all, simply have experience; we are entrusted with it. We must do something—make something—with it. A story, we sense, is the only possible habitation for the burden of our witnessing." —Patricia Hampl, *I Could Tell You Stories: Sojourns in the Land of Memory*

In the summer of 2004, after nearly three decades as a journalist for newspapers and magazines in Texas and California, I became a staff writer for *The Washington Post.* Hiring someone my age was unusual for the Post, but my primary task for the paper was also unusual. Along with four other veteran journalists of wide experience, I would be an obituary writer. My colleagues and I would take one of the lowlier beats on most newspaper staffs—where rookie reporters traditionally learn the mundane but necessary habits of accuracy and thoroughness—and transform it. We would write about the dead and in the process re-create lives in all the depth and fullness we could summon. We would be writing, not memorials, but biographies in miniature—about saints and scoundrels, about the well known and the unknown. We would seek to capture—on deadline, of course—the particularity of a person's existence in all its richness and idiosyncrasy.

In my years of experience as a journalist, I had written a total of three obituaries—two for the *New York Times* about Texas political figures and one about my father for his hometown newspaper. For that reason alone, I was apprehensive during my first few days at the Post. What do you say to a stranger, I wondered, who has just experienced the loss of a spouse, a child, a dear friend? How do you capture a life in twenty inches or less of newsprint?

I soon realized that I had no reason to be concerned. I discovered that something intriguing almost always takes place during the process of collaborating with a family member on re-creating a person's life. Since I have not known the person, the family member isn't expecting me to feel the same sense of loss, which frees me to ask questions, to listen intently, and to guide the spouse or the parent or the sibling through a process of remembering. They tell me stories, recall memories, share the particles of a person's existence. We even laugh together over the silly things that happened through the years. Instead of concentrating on a death, in other words, we attempt the biographer's task. We do our best to bring a person back to life.

In *Evacuation Plan: A Novel from the Hospice*, Joe O'Connell recounts in fictional form a similar opportunity. Matt, his narrator, a screenwriter scouting for material in a place where people have gone to die, is at first reluctant to intrude on the rapidly dwindling moments of time at the end of a person's life. He feels bumbling and exploitative, frets that he's becoming a "grief junkie." But gradually, as he drops by the hospice every day or so, as he sits at the bedside of patients and teases out their stories, he learns a lesson similar to what I have learned as an obituary writer. He discovers that in the shared process of making something of their experience, of shaping a story out of the raw materials of their existence, the people he comes to know at the hospice become truly and fully alive.

The stories Matt hears aren't always pretty. Far from it. But for the people telling those stories, the act of sharing their experiences with a willing listener gives even the most troubled lives a richness and dignity they would not otherwise have had. "Death without a history is the cruelest joke of all," Matt observes at one point. He's determined not to let that happen, if at all possible.

One of his favorite patients is a garrulous old man named Charlie Wright who invariably has wonderful stories to share, as well as life lessons worth heeding. "And it is good you are here on this side for him," a nurse assures Matt. "He thinks your writing is his immortality."

It is, of course. For Charlie Wright, for all of us, memory—memory shaped and shared—is the true reality. It is our immortality.

Joe O'Connell's fictional screenwriter has one advantage over the real-life obituary writer, in that he's able to meet the people he writes about before death asserts its tyranny. What we have in common, however, is something quite profound: We're both dealing with death, but we're writing about life. *Evacuation Plan* itself may be set in a hospice, but it is, in fact, a rich and compelling book of life.

Joe Holley
Chevy Chase, Md.

For Frieda and Kay.

Bon voyage, ladies,

and thanks for the pie.

THE SCREENWRITER

ANNIE MAY LEADS ME down the hospice hallway and into a partially open door. Mr. Wright's eyes are closed, but they flash open at our arrival.

"Am I dead yet?" he booms. "Is this a pair of angels sent to whisk me on my way to the heavens where I'll be bathed by dainty virgins and talk philosophy and smoke cigars with Mr. Freud?"

"No, not dead," Annie May says. "Ugly, maybe, but not dead."

"Annie May." His hair is white, thick, and looks to be recently combed. His voice drops into the disk jockey zone. "She's a goddess. Come to make an honest man of me. Is this your son, Annie?"

"Wrong color, Mr. Wright."

"He is a tad pale. The tadpole is a tad pale. Get your son some sun!" He winks and gestures for me to grab a seat. "But a fetching lad. So you beat me to her. Gigolo. Sly dog."

"This is our filmmaker," Annie May says.

"Ah, the creative genius has come to pick my brain. Better do it while I've still got something left. Sit, boy. Sit."

I pull a chair up by the bed, but the seat is already taken by an artificial leg. I feel goose bumps raise on my arm.

"Diabetes," Mr. Wright says. "At least I have one leg to stand on. Toss it in the corner, boy."

I pick it up gently and feel its heft. The shoe and sock on it creep me out as I drop it by the wall. Not much to the room: a bed, a couch, two overstuffed chairs; sink by the wall and a small refrigerator. But it's more homey than a hospital room.

Annie May laughs at me again and the old man who is 70, 75, though he acts younger, joins in. He's wearing pressed baby–blue pajamas and the pink of his cheeks sharply contrasts to the white hair.

"I've named it Henrietta after my first wife," he says and points at the leg. "I never liked Henrietta. But she gave me two strapping boys and one heavenly daughter."

"Is diabetes why you're here?" I settle in the chair.

"Diabetes and the Triple A," he says. "I'm a full–fledged member. Asthma, arteriosclerosis, and arrogance. Heavy on the latter."

"Don't let him fool you." Annie May stands over us with one hand on her hip. "He's a lover, not a fighter."

"Annie May!" he says. "I'll make an honest woman of you yet, you little flirt."

He turns toward me and offers a hand. It's warm to the touch. Not what I expected from a dying man. Little of this place is what I'd expected.

"Name's Charlie Wright. No relation to Frank Lloyd Wright, but we shared the same business, and the ladies here like to delude themselves that I'm an artiste. Sorry, Annie May. I just put up ugly boxy buildings for the government and a school or three. A company man. Not an artist like this young man."

"Some would argue whether movies are art," I say.

"Don't let the bastards get you down. What's your name?"

"Matt. I guess you could say I'm here in search of a good story. Can you tell me what it's like to be in this place?"

"Cream of the crop," he says. "Everything is aces at the hospice. Better than that damn hospital any day. But you don't need a story; you need a model. That's what we do in my field. Then we can see what a building will look like in three dimensions."

He cups his hands as if cradling a ball.

"Closed structure." His hand unfolds. "Open structure."

He looks at me as if waiting for some kind of sign that I'm getting it. I put on that nodding smile I used with my own father when he started lecturing.

"Matt, Matt, Matt. A closed structure doesn't change. That's death. An open structure has three dimensions, like a model house, and is open to change."

"I see." But I still don't quite get his point.

"Don't sweat the story, boy! The moment you think you've got a lasso on it, it's going to change."

Okay, I get it. I need to let the story come to me.

"So that's how you see death?" I ask.

"We're always afraid of change," he says. "You better not remodel one of my buildings, bub. But lack of change is what should scare us."

"Are you ready for the end, Mr. Wright?"

"Name's Charlie," he says. "The end?"

"Death," I say. "I wonder what it's like to be facing death."

His face gets serious, and his left hand reaches out to caress the bed's metal railing.

"Dying ..." It comes out of him more as a question than a statement. "By golly, I guess I am going to die. Imagine that." His eyes turn first to Annie May then toward me. "No worries, folks. I've got it mostly figured out."

"Mr. Wright looks tired," Annie May says and motions for us to leave.

The old man nods.

"Come back and see me, boy. We'll find that story yet."

"It's a date."

In the hallway, Annie May kisses me on the cheek.

"What was that for?"

"You did Mr. Wright a favor. You reminded him that his journey is close, and he's got to prepare."

"What now?"

"You're ready, Matt. Time to fly solo. I'll be around somewhere if you need me."

∽∽∽

I knock at Room Five and wait a second before entering. The woman in the bed has reddish-yellow hair that is shaved away on one side of her head, which is large and flabby. Her eyes are vacant and don't focus as I approach her bedside.

"Mrs. Fiola? How you doing?" I say the words slowly and loudly.

Nothing. No change, then I realize I've asked one of the questions Annie May said don't matter at the hospice.

"I'm wondering if you can tell me about your life, Mrs. Fiola."

Her eyes find me for a second, then spin away.

"Not a bad life." Her voice is soft, younger than she looks.

"You have children?"

"No, never married. An ugly duckling."

"What kind of career did you have?"

She pauses as if in deep thought.

"Worked at the post office sorting mail." The words are a mumbled soup. "In a bookstore. Nothing much."

"Was there a best moment to your life?"

She licks her lips, and after a few seconds her eyes clear and focus on mine.

"In the Army. Vietnam. Doing paperwork at hospitals. Front lines. One day a doctor comes in. Pregnant woman. Says needs help. I didn't know what to do. Coming out so slow. Head pops out. He says catch the baby. I look down and here it comes. Falls right in my hands. A baby girl."

"That's beautiful."

I take out my pad and scribble her words on it. Her eyes start to wander again. I have to speak up before I lose her.

"You believe in heaven, Mrs. Fiola? Hell?"

She props her hand and forearm straight up in front of her, and the arm wavers like a gas gauge in a car.

"Done some bad things, some good," she says. "Hope my balance is over the proper way. Figure I'm right on the thin line."

Her eyes start to cloud again. Her arm drops, and her head falls back to the pillow. Done.

I tiptoe into the hallway and try to shut the door behind me as silently as possible. A man with bloodshot eyes comes out of another room. Inside I see another elderly woman. She is awake and smiling toward someone else. All I can see are his hands.

"Hey," the bloodshot guy says in greeting. His clothes are wrinkled and his breath reeks of stale beer. ☙

THE GUY IN THE HALL

I HAD JUST TURNED late fifty–something and what little sleep I could manage took place in a bedroom that used to be part of a sprawling wooden porch. Knowing I was approaching fifty and that certain death waited on the horizon was bad enough, but moving back into my parents' house—the house I grew up in—brought on major anxiety attacks. Within those walls, there was no way I could dodge the fact that I'd let my life slip by in a swift flow of idiotic failures. The ghosts of my past circled over my bed at night while I curled into the fetal position and fought to breathe. There was Mother winding up a musical platter that slowly spun my little brother Tim's fifth birthday cake while playing "Happy Birthday to You." Tim staring with anticipation at the presents piled next to the cake. Dad laughing at his two boys, cigar smoke floating from his tired mouth. There was Mother crying without expression the day my father keeled over at his office and died. I was fifteen, Dad was fifty–five. And there, me, sucking that one drop of nectar out of a honeysuckle and letting the sickly-sweet smell fill my nose.

The sad truth was that the past became more and more inviting when compared to the present. Despite the claustrophobia of it, I needed to be alone with myself. I had to look for once face to face at Patrick Ott—a sad, divorced father of none who grew bored with any job or relationship he had to put up with for more than two years running. Patrick, a guy who was secretly glad his seventy–year–old mother was dying in a hospice so he could claim her home as his own, all the while watching his own body begin to bloat and fall apart. Looking in the mirror at this pathetic, balding husk of a human being, it became harder and harder to believe he was me.

Maybe he wasn't.

Mother had never remarried. She taught Sunday school and did volunteer work at the veterans' hospital. Dad was fully vested in the profit–sharing plan at the plant where he was head of purchasing. Mother had taken that tidy sum and a hefty insurance payoff—my father was the type who selected his clothing for the following day before he went to bed at night—invested it wisely and lived off the interest.

By the time Dad died, I was getting stoned as soon as I got home from school. Back then—God, I sound like Mother talking about the good old days—you could buy a really good lid for $20, an okay one for $10. I hung out with Brett Strunk, a reed-thin guy from the neighborhood. All the chicks liked Strunk. He had a smooth patter and his rich parents bought him a fancy red Mustang convertible. Even Mother liked him.

"That young man knows the value of friendly conversation," she said once before running to the bathroom to touch up that White Rain concrete mix she sprayed on her hair. "Smile, Patrick. Don't be so serious."

Strunk and I partied together pretty constantly for those next three years. We'd hang over at my place on the porch. It was huge and overlooked this little creek I used to play in when I was a kid. We'd bring chicks over, pull my stereo out, and smoke pot until the tops of our heads opened up and let the stars in. Strunk went on to college and we lost touch.

Mother wanted me to go to college, even said she'd pay for it. But I got a job selling electronics down at the mall. Back then I could sell anything to anybody. Decked out in my blue blazer, slacks, and tie, I'd put on a cocky attitude and convince customers that I was an electronics guru. They bought it. I was making decent money and I had one deadly stereo—at below cost. Strunk sold me his convertible before he left for Ivy League land, and life was cruising.

ಌ ಌ ಌ

Tim was the one who told me about Mother. She'd wandered off from the house for the umpteenth time and a cop delivered Mother to him after finding her naked, perched on the roof of a neighbor's car. The cop said she kept calmly repeating: "I wasn't expecting company today." Tim's wife, Madelyn, is one hundred percent bitch and she was not at all pleased to have the unexpected company.

The Alzheimer's combined with all of her other diseases and disorders were sealing the deal. The doctors gave her months to live at most.

"Here's the deal, Patrick," Tim said with a sigh. "Take care of the house and visit her regularly. I'll pay to put Mom in the hospice."

"You mean a death house, little brother. Call it what it is."

He stared at me coldly. "I call it facing the facts. You can't keep sleeping on my living room couch, and we don't want the kids to have to watch Mother die." His look told me all I needed to know—this was not negotiable. Madelyn had put her foot down.

ᘓᘓᘓ

I was twenty–one when I met Jordie. She was a sales associate in Swain's Department Store in the cosmetics section. Everybody who worked at the mall took their breaks at this little cafe that specialized in imported coffee. One day I was in there sitting with Frank Pearman from Land o' Luggage and he started hitting mercilessly on a little brunette with bangs hanging down in her eyes. I'll never forget the angel drawing on her t–shirt, and the way it fluttered when she laughed in Pearman's face. Then she slipped me her business card on the way out. I think she did it just to piss Pearman off, but I wasn't going to pass up the opportunity.

Jordie Calderon was nineteen, wild and beautiful, and she damn well knew it. I put a bottle of sangria in my Styrofoam ice chest and took her to the drive–in movie. She smelled so damn good, like sunshine and baby shampoo. I have no idea what movie was playing. Don't get me wrong, we mainly just talked. About everything. The future, God, love, school, parents, underwear—everything. There was something about her that was so familiar, so natural.

"You know what I like about you, Patrick?" she said and kissed me lightly on the ear.

"No, what?"

"I think you have a passion for life." She moved her body closer to mine. "You're going to do things. I can feel it."

Kissing Jordie the first time was the best moment of my life. I stared into her eyes and their glow seeped into me, warming my chest, maybe my soul. We both knew that it wasn't just another grope in the dark. We were in love and I was too young to know what that truly meant.

ᘓᘓᘓ

My parents' house didn't look much different than it had when I was a little kid. That same 1950s furniture Beaver Cleaver would have loved. The first thing I did after lugging my bags in was to open every single window in the place. The stench of age wouldn't let loose of my childhood home.

About seven years back, Mother had the idea of walling in the porch and renting it as an apartment. Like I said, it was huge. I cleaned up the mess left by the last tenants and moved out there. Somehow I couldn't see moving directly back into my past, and the porch was at least changed.

I'd been sleeping on Tim's couch for about a month before going to Mother's. I couldn't think of a soul I still knew in town. I came close to calling my ex–girlfriend Vickie to see if there was any chance she might take me back one more time, but I knew that would be pointless. I had found the locks changed and all of my worldly goods stacked on the front porch when I'd returned from the 7–Eleven with a fresh pack of Merit 100s.

"Come back when you have a job," Vickie said from behind the door. I couldn't get another word out of her. Vickie is five years older than me and managed the apartment complex we'd lived in. She was the last in a long line of people I'd treated like shit.

I guess Tim would add Mother to the list, but I don't really see how he can blame me for her dying. Anyway, the point is that back in my parents' house I had way too much time to think. Mother had an old Volvo, but for some reason the thought of driving it gave me chest pains. It felt like my rib cage was slowly shrinking. I was constantly wiping the sweat off my upper lip. Instead of driving, I started walking. Morning, night, afternoon, whenever the memories started closing in too tightly, I walked. I walked past my old school, Pemberton Court Elementary. I walked past First Presbyterian Church where I used to play tag football with Strunk and the guys. I walked past the houses of friends who had long since moved away. I couldn't walk fast enough.

⁂

One Sunday night about two weeks after moving home, I walked down to the 7–Eleven for a twelve pack of Budweiser and I drank it while going through some of Mother's things. There was this old cabinet my father had made when he was young. Dad wanted to become an artist and it showed in the carvings he did on the sides of the cabinet. On one side a sailboat floated slowly by, on another an Indian chief stared sternly out. Mom loved that cabinet. She was always polishing the wood. That wood glowed in a way Dad never quite could for her.

Inside the cabinet were a bunch of Dad's old Dutch Masters cigar boxes, each with a date written on it with a felt marker. Mother was a stickler for organization. I grabbed 1960 and a fresh beer, and went back to the porch.

The cigar box was sealed with a piece of yellowed Scotch tape. The tape felt greasy and slipped right off. I lifted the box over my head and poured photographs onto the bed around me like huge confetti.

I made a game of picking the photos up randomly. Here were three little girls clutching dolls and a stoic boy in overalls sitting in a row in the middle of a field of bluebonnets. By my feet was a studio portrait of a smiling man wearing a bow tie. Who were these people? On my left a shot of my father as a young man—somebody must have put it in the wrong box. He and another soldier were clowning, their elbows resting on the shoulders of a smiling woman. I realized I was now older than this man who would become my father. The thought brought a wave of nausea over me.

And Christmas. At least half of the photos my family took were either at Christmas or on someone's birthday. I could trace my growth through photos of me standing in front of almost identical Christmas trees. All that changed were my size and the present I held proudly up. In 1960 it was a Lone Ranger pistol a five–year–old me aimed at the camera. I knew waiting in other cigar boxes were images of me holding a transistor radio, a G.I. Joe, a tennis racket. I started to wonder if Mother had those gifts all piled away somewhere downstairs. I would open a door and out they would fall. Maybe Dad would be standing behind them, smiling.

∽ ∽ ∽

I woke up three hours later drooling on a photo of my cousin Mary wearing a top hat and tap shoes, her arms stretched out at her sides. The left side of my head throbbed and I noticed my arms were trembling. I'd been cooped up in the house far too long. So, at two in the morning, I went out walking again.

It was misting lightly and the air was cool and thick. I walked without a plan, ducking down alleys and crossing through parks. I saw a few lighted windows, but most of the neighborhood seemed to be asleep. The mist sprinkled my face and I realized the headache was receding.

After about forty–five minutes, I decided to circle back to the house. My head felt better, but my legs were tiring. I was okay until I came upon the church and that goddamn cross. It towered over me, painted black but eerily illuminated from below. That cross scared the shit out of me when I was a kid. An older guy from down the street, Jimmy McDuffee, had told us it was alive and ate children. We believed him then, and I wasn't sure I didn't believe him still.

It was crazy. I was almost ready to run away like a scared five–year–old, but I made myself walk past it. Then I heard something move in the shadows ahead. A tiny voice was mumbling. All I could understand was "hombre," or it might have been "I'm brave." I wasn't sure. I couldn't quite make him out, but it looked to be a small boy. As I came closer I saw he was facing away from me. He had a holster around his waist and was wearing a cowboy hat. What was this child doing out in the middle of the night? The possibilities made my stomach churn.

"Bang! Bang! You're dead. I shot you. You have to die now," he said and turned toward me.

I couldn't make out his face, but he was dressed entirely in black.

"Aren't you out kind of late, kid?" I asked when I got close enough. I could feel my heart thumping loudly, but it was like it belonged to someone else. "What's your name?"

He pointed the gun at me.

"You're the bad guy. You robbed the bank and I'm taking you in."

This was too weird, so I did something even weirder. I pulled three fingers to my palm and held out my thumb and forefinger to form a gun. A black mask covered the boy's eyes, but I still recognized him. I shot at him with my hand.

"Gotcha," I said, laughing hysterically. "You'll never take me alive."

The boy frowned. "But you're dead. I shot you first."

Then he ran back into the shadows and vanished. All I could think about was his outfit and how much I liked the gold embroidery that snaked along his shirt and hat. I wanted one just like it. Maybe I was spending too much time alone, but that cowboy suit was all I could think about as I walked home and crawled back into bed.

I woke up around noon and rifled through the pictures until I found it. There he, I, was, pointing the gun at the camera, dressed entirely in black. I tried to convince myself it was a dream, but that didn't explain my sore feet. I lit up a joint and pulled the covers up to my chin.

ಌ ಌ ಌ

My marriage to Jordie had lasted exactly five years, three months and eighteen days. She'd been taking an occasional course at the community college when I first met her, and she'd talked me into signing up, too. That didn't last long. It had reminded me too much of high school.

"You have to think about the future some time," Jordie said.

But I'd been hired by the biggest electronics chain in town and was pulling in a pretty hefty commission. Sales had become my life.

Then Jordie got a real estate license and started making real cash. We had talked about having a kid, but somehow never got around to it. I had to admit I was getting jealous of the life she led apart from me. If she wasn't at work, she was in a class or meeting her new friends for happy hour. Some of her new friends were men.

"He's just a friend, baby," I can still hear her saying. "Relax."

We each tried to save the marriage in our own ways. I started bringing her flowers a lot and I even signed up for a French class with her. I wasn't good at languages. Jordie started roping me into these "serious talks." She would sit me down at the dining room table and force me to talk about our relationship.

"What do you want, Patrick?" she'd ask, her arms locked at her chest, her face turning pink. "Tell me. Anything."

How could I tell her when I didn't know myself? I couldn't believe someone like Jordie would want to be with me. I was driving Strunk's Mustang and I was living his life, too. But deep down I wasn't Strunk and I knew I never would be. I couldn't tell her that, so I didn't say anything.

I was scared to death of losing Jordie, so I started clinging tightly to her. I tried to pull her down to where I thought I was. I'm almost certain of the exact moment I lost her.

"This real estate thing is not going to cut it, you know," I said. "You're trying to be this executive woman, but that's not you. You're going to fuck up."

"Why don't you get a life and quit trying to tell me how to live mine," she said. She was crying. I could see the distance in her eyes.

ঌ ঌ ঌ

Three weeks later, Jordie moved out. Six months after that I quit my job and moved to California. I had to get away.

ঌ ঌ ঌ

The next night I went to sleep staring at the photograph of the kid in the Lone Ranger outfit. I slept straight through. In the morning, I walked around the neighborhood again and nothing happened. It had to have been a dream after all. There was no other explanation.

ঌ ঌ ঌ

California was my fantasy. Beaches, movie stars, models, money. I'd moved there with a thousand dollars in cash and Strunk's Mustang. The Mustang died a week after I arrived and the cash hadn't lasted much longer. I got a job working the night shift in a convenience store. That lasted about six months. I fell asleep in the basement storage area one night and the store was robbed. They took twenty cases of beer and all of the beef jerky.

The next seven years went by in a blur. I worked in a string of unmemorable jobs and dated women whose names and faces I mostly can't recall. I started drinking a lot, and I became afraid of something I couldn't quite put into words.

I hit rock bottom—or so I thought—at age thirty–four when I found myself working as a parking attendant at one of Carmel's finest restaurants. I was hustling five–dollar tips from guys my own age, driving their Porsches, Corvettes, and Cadillacs for two minutes at a time. One day I just went up to my boss, a blond beach boy ten years younger than me, handed in my polyester vest and bow tie, and decided to move home.

ঌ ঌ ঌ

I opened the cabinet again on Tuesday. I was planning to put 1960 away, but I thought, what the hell, and decided to look through some more pictures. I took out what was probably the banner year of my life—1969— and sat down on the couch to lose myself in the past.

My father stood next to our new car. It was what he had always wanted. The Cadillac was a symbol that he'd finally made it. I stood by him next to the open driver's side door. Mother was on the other side with her arm around Tim's shoulders. We were a family. The car was still under extended warranty the day Dad died.

I thumbed quickly through the other pictures. I knew what I was looking for. Yes. There I was holding a Joe Namath football up to the camera, the tree behind sparkling with colored bulbs and tinsel. The boy in the photograph had curiously come back into style. He was smiling and young, shoulder–length hair parted on the side and falling into his eyes. He was the one who scored touchdowns and made B's in all his classes. The one his parents were proud of.

I woke up on the couch with a start. I couldn't breathe and my heart raced. Night fear—I'd had it off and on for years but it always left me sure I had barely beaten death. I threw on a coat and headed out the door. I had no idea what time it was.

The moon was full and the cloudless sky sparkled. I walked fast with my head down. My own body was attacking me; it wouldn't give me peace. I walked faster and faster until the anxiety drained away. When I looked up I was by the elementary school. I walked past the bike rack and peered into a window. Construction paper cutouts of bears, stars, and letters of the alphabet covered the walls at random. The desks were lined up in rows facing away from me.

"Hey, old man, go long."

The voice came from somewhere behind me. I turned around and saw him, leaning on a fence, bouncing a football in his hand. His hair covered his eyes. I knew I should have been scared, but this time I wasn't. I loped down the field. My lungs felt young and pink. I turned my head over my left shoulder and watched the ball arrive as if in slow motion. I pulled it down with both hands and tumbled to the ground. Touchdown.

I fought to catch my breath and started feeling old and scared again. He was standing over me when I looked up.

"Nice catch for a geezer." He smiled.

He was wearing one of the Monkees T–shirts that Uncle Will had given Tim and me for Christmas that year. This time I wasn't going to let him get away. Calm, I had to stay calm.

"You throw a mean spiral," I said. "You play high school ball?"

"Nah, next year. I'm only in junior high."

"What position?"

"Wide receiver. I'm the best. Nobody can catch me."

His wide grin told me it was true, he was the best. He was beautiful. What happened to us? I realized in a year his father would be dead and slowly, ever so slowly, the demons would begin to close in.

"Don't ever let them catch you, Patrick," I said. "You hear me? Just keep your eye on the ball."

His head jerked when I spoke his name, then the smile crept back.

"Sure, man. I'm going all the way. Hey, how about tossing me one?"

He flowed across the field like water down a mountain stream. Natural. I cocked back my arm and let it sail. The football hung in the air for an ungodly time, then floated into his hands.

"Touchdown!" he yelled, his arms pointing at the stars.

A car pulled up to the curb and the door swung open. He waved from across the schoolyard.

"Later, alligator," he said.

I started to run for him, but the door slammed shut and the car drove away. I could tell by the taillights that it was a Cadillac.

ꝏ ꝏ ꝏ

Coming back home after all those years in California wasn't as easy as I had expected. I had heard that Jordie was living with an older guy, a divorced attorney with kids in high school. I stayed with Mother for a few days, but she was renting the porch out to some ultra–conservative college students and they made me nervous. Mother didn't know what to make of me. She kept giving me these little pep talks about having a positive attitude.

"Don't waste your life, Patrick," she said, with this aging Junior League grin. "Find your dream and follow it."

Tim put me up for a while, but that was tense, too. I noticed that Madelyn hid her purse when I was around. Sammy, their little boy, was great. He treated me like a real person.

Fortunately, I got out of that situation pretty quick. Tim gave me a suit and drove me to job leads. Within two weeks I was hired as a photographer working out of a shopping mall. It was almost like old times, only instead of hawking electronics I was trying to make babies smile. I didn't know much about photography, but I lied and learned.

Walking to the coffee shop one afternoon, I thought I saw Jordie. This woman moved in the floaty way Jordie had. She went into Victoria's Secret and I didn't dare follow.

I met Vickie on the job. She brought her little girl Sara in for a sitting about a month before Christmas. Vickie and I were comfortable together and that was about all either of us could ask. Sara's father had quit his construction job and left town two years before.

What I liked best about Vickie was holding her in my arms. That was better than the best sex I ever had, except maybe with Jordie. Why I had to fuck it up I couldn't explain. Vickie and I started going to bars whenever we could talk someone in the apartment complex into babysitting. Then I started going by myself. At work, a few mothers complained about the alcohol I breathed on their children. I was fired. Again.

ᔕ ᔕ ᔕ

I ran all the way home. God, there was no denying it this time. It had happened twice, and maybe it would happen again. Something special was being given to me. The photograph was on the couch where I'd left it. It was me. I was that boy with the cocky grin and the great hands. I could be that way again, I was sure of it. I didn't drink that night, and I slept like a baby.

ᔕ ᔕ ᔕ

The next afternoon, I put the photographs back in the 1969 cigar box and watched Mother's TV for a while. I was waiting for the right time. There was no rush. I dozed on the couch, waking long enough to catch snippets from reruns of *Laverne and Shirley*—Lenny and Squiggy with another hare–brained scheme—and *Rockford Files*—another client turns up dead.

By ten o'clock I couldn't stand it anymore. I went to the cabinet and pulled out 1976, our bicentennial year, the year I met Jordie. The box was almost empty. Dad was the big picture taker in the family and after he died no one cared to take his place. There was one envelope in the box. Christmas photos. Tim's and my hair still covered our ears, but our bellbottoms had slimmed to flares. The Christmas tree was a small, live one this time. I was holding up lamb's wool seat covers, one draped over each arm. That was the year I grew a mustache.

In the next few hours I memorized everything about that photograph. The way I tilted my head toward the camera. The wadded–up wrapping paper behind me. That scrawny tree. I had to remember it all.

The TV screen was a mass of static when I woke up. It was four in the morning and it was time. I felt alive.

I walked out the door. Through the mist I saw a red Mustang convertible idling at the curb. The passenger door swung open and the driver said, "Hop in." I was not afraid.

"Thanks for the lift," I said. The car was immaculate. The seat cushions felt soft and familiar on my back.

"No problem." His mustache turned up at the corners to form a smile.

"Say, if I didn't know better I'd think I was in Brett Strunk's car."

He nodded. "You don't know better and it is, or used to be, his. Are you a relative of Strunk's or something?"

"Or something."

Neither of us talked for a while. He turned on the radio. Peter Frampton asked the musical question, "Do you feel like I do?"

I couldn't stop staring at him. All that hair. It was so maddening the way it had slowly thinned until my scalp started peeking through. He was so young. God, I missed him.

"Sorry about Dad, Patrick," I said. "You doing okay?"

He chewed on his bottom lip. "I guess. It's tough, you know? The old man got on my nerves a lot, but he was cool. I guess I have to grow up now. What a drag."

He fell silent. Peter Frampton played the mouth organ and the recorded audience hooted. "Do–you–feel–like–I–do?"

"Are you in love, Patrick?" I asked.

He beamed. "Does it show? Yeah, I guess I am. She's incredible. We have everything in common. We like the same things. It's little stuff, like we both love ice cream. That probably sounds stupid, but it somehow matters. You know. You're probably married, right?"

I had to stifle a laugh.

"I used to be," I said.

"Oh, sorry, man. Was it a bad scene?"

"Yeah, I fucked up. I guess I learned you don't need money or a red convertible to deserve love. You can do it on your own. I mean, I guess. I've never actually gotten that far myself."

"Drag," he said. "But then again it doesn't hurt to have a little help. If you know Strunk, you know that."

"Yeah," I said, and realized he wasn't going to listen to me. How could he if he was to become me? I was getting anxious again. Why was I here if not to help him, to stop him from doing what I had done? I stared out the window into the black night. I noticed my hands were shaking again.

"Hey, Patrick, got any advice for a lonely old man?"

He cocked his head, just like in the photograph.

"Well, first off, stay on that side of the car. Nah, just kidding, man. Old? I guess I always figured you get old when you run out of options. But there's always options. You ain't dead yet."

I'd come a long way for advice I could have gotten from a fortune cookie, but you take what you can get.

"I think this is my stop," I said.

I opened the door and I was in front of Mother's house.

"Patrick," I said, offering him my hand. "Treat her right."

He squeezed my hand so tightly that a tear leaked from the corner of my left eye.

He said, "Always. Just like you would." ☙

for attention. Overstuffed couches in bright colors here and there. On the walls, paintings of boats lolling on an open sea.

This is the side for the living. Where the relatives and friends cry. Where the smiles are painted on before we venture down the hall to the other leg of the H–shaped house.

ꟷ ꟷ ꟷ

Three days have passed since I first ventured in, and everything has changed. Annie May is off, the nurse on duty is a stunning blonde, half the names on the dry erase board are different, and a tuxedoed violinist is performing classical music by the nurse's station.

In the hallway a few patients watch the performance—a woman from her wheelchair and a man from a hospital bed.

"Did they die?" I ask the nurse and point. At first glance she looks college age, but fine lines around her eyes tell me she's much older. She glances at my nametag and seems satisfied I'm legit.

"Some. Always some. Anyone in particular?"

"Mr. Wright, Mrs. Fiola."

She examines a chart. "Mrs. Fiola discharged."

"You mean she died?"

"No, they wanted her at home. Freaky, eh? Never can guess who'll be here tomorrow, dead or alive. Keeps us hopping."

"Mr. Wright?"

"Charlie's been asking for you, Matt. Let's go say hello. I'm Mary."

We pass the woman in the wheelchair. On her lap is a tray of chocolate candies, and her hand is struggling in slow motion to grasp one of them. I reach to help her, but Mary swats my hand away.

"She doesn't need your help."

Mary raps on the door, but pushes in before Mr. Wright can reply.

"Company calling."

Mr. Wright is paler than last time, but he opens one eyelid and checks us out.

"My daughter?"

"No, the screenwriter."

The other eye pops open, and he waves us in.

A compact man, slighter older than me, is sitting in a chair with a Bible in his hand. In starched shirt and chinos, he looks like he just arrived from a semi–casual office.

Mary grabs Mr. Wright's shoulder and props his torso up so she can fluff the pillows.

"Ah," Wright says. "God loves us invalids. She even smells of homegrown peaches."

He reaches for her hair, but Mary pushes his hand away.

"Hands off the fruit."

Wright laughs and his son looks away toward the window.

"Did I tell you my daughter's a writer, too?"

"I could never have the patience for that," Mary says. "I get my kicks teasing old men."

"Score!" Wright says. "Now if my son would get off his duff and ask for your phone number."

"Dad," the man says.

"I'm spoken for, Mr. Wright, and a bit old for your son. But thanks for the offer. Buzz if you need anything."

Once she's gone, Wright's bravado recedes.

"I've been making phone calls." He doesn't look at me or his son as he says it. "Tying up loose ends. This is my youngest boy Bob. Meet the movie maker come to immortalize me."

Bob offers a tight–lipped grin.

"Dad, I'm going to get some air and let you guys talk."

"Fair enough," Mr. Wright says. "Take your time. Matt and I'll have a man–to–man."

The son waves his hand high as he disappears.

"I'm getting on his nerves," Mr. Wright says. "Can't blame him. I'm an old pain in the ass. You know how it is with fathers and sons."

"Sure," I say. "I remember at least. I lost my father a few years back."

"Ah, hope it's not catching. But I'm afraid it is. What'd your old man do for a living?"

"Salesman."

"Backbone of our country," Mr. Wright says. "I never understood them, but they make all the . . ."

His eyes concentrate on the ceiling.

"Rhymes with honey. Funny. Money! That's it."

He drapes his hands on top of his head.

"Sometimes I can't find the words anymore, Matt. They drift away. For a blowhard like me that's an ugly irony."

More has changed about Mr. Wright than I'd originally thought. He seems tired and frail.

"Your son doesn't look a lot like you."

I'm trying my best to change the subject.

"Or act like me," he says. "I love the boy deeply, but I confess to not understanding him a whit. Somehow it works out. We get past the silence."

"Silence?"

"Yeah, when we can't figure out what to say to each other. After the divorce I used to drive two hundred miles every morning, just so I could take the kids to school. Prove my mettle as a dad. With my girl Carla it was fine. Bob was a quiet little mouse. Lots of anger. The silence was deafening."

"As a fellow child of divorced parents, I can bet he appreciated you being there all the same," I say.

Mr. Wright lets loose a throaty laugh.

"Ah, parents. We screw up our children royally, or at least that's the way they see it. My father was a bastard. Big, quiet, John Wayne type. Worked with his hands. Didn't talk much, but he taught me to fight. I tried the same with Bob. Kids were picking on him at the elementary school. It didn't take."

"At least you tried," I say.

"I hate to trouble you, boy, but I need a … it's in that closet over there."

He points across the room and I go investigate.

"The thing for catching it."

I can tell he's searching for the right word again. I hold up a trashcan.

"No!" His frustration comes out in a yelp. "The goddamn metal…

I show him a bedpan.

"That's it!"

He takes it from me and holds it in his hand.

"Bedpan," he says as if trying to memorize the word. "Doesn't that cheese you off? I can't even remember the name for a bedpan."

I nod.

"One day all of this will be yours."

"If I'm lucky."

"Correct," Mr. Wright says. "Now leave me a little privacy for the dirty work."

ↀ ↀ ↀ

The music has stopped but the patients still stare at the spot the violinist once occupied. Bob sits on the couch by the copy machine. He waves me over.

"Thanks for giving me a break," he says. "I love the old man, but sometimes it's a bit much."

"Are you spending a lot of time here?"

"Practically moved in. I'm between projects now, so the timing is good."

His words are slow and deliberate. He takes off his glasses and rubs them on his shirt before replacing them.

"Your father is a great guy," I say.

"Yeah. He seems to like you a lot. He likes having people to talk to."

"What kind of projects do you do?"

"Architecture."

"The family business," I say. "You must make your father proud."

"Some days," he says and places the glasses back on his nose. "Some days." ↀ

THE SON

EMILY CALLED BOB BO–BO and brought him invisible cookies. Chocolate chips were his favorite—he often munched a bag of the real ones while studying for his architecture classes, crumbs littering his desk.

Bob pulled her seatbelt tight and prepared for his job as driver/child exchanger, a fragile thread connecting divorced parents who hated each other.

"I've got a surprise, Bo–Bo," she said, tucking her chin to her chest and opening her eyes wide.

"Is it an elephant?"

"Silly, an elephant's too big."

"A new car?"

"No, I like this one. It's green."

Emily reached into a pocket at the waist of her little plaid dress. "Hold out your hand, Bo–Bo."

"That's a little one," Bob said, staring into his palm before raising the invisible cookie to his mouth and chewing. "Yuck! Licorice."

Emily shook her head from side to side and giggled. "No, it's not." She checked her pocket. "That's the wrong one. Here."

Once it was in his mouth Bob knew. "Chocolate chip?"

Emily nodded.

As they pulled away from Emily's father's house, Bob started to wonder. "Who was the licorice cookie for?"

"For my Daddy."

"Oh, does he like licorice?"

"No."

ഗ ഗ ഗ

It had taken Bob four hours to drive from his apartment near the university in Austin to Tom Hariman's beach house on Padre Island. Now he was fulfilling the duties of his part–time job—running the South Texas scenery in reverse with Emily beside him. Bob remembered Emily's Dad and how it had been immediately obvious that he was an engineer. He wore a fishing jumpsuit that reminded Bob of the orange ones on the G.I. Joe doll he had as a kid, and Mr. Hariman's toupee looked about as realistic as G.I. Joe's hair.

"I know Melinda hired you, Bob," Mr. Hariman had said when Bob arrived to take Emily. "I hope you don't mind, but I did a little checking on you. I called some fellers teaching down in the architecture department and they said you were a cool dude. Some of them knew your father. Hell, we all know the good work his firm does."

He was good at leaving us behind, too, Bob thought. Mr. Hariman grinned and moved his hands in a slow, deliberate way that reminded Bob of his own father.

"Thank you, sir."

"Well, it's nothing personal. We got ourselves a unique situation." Bob stared up the front of Mr. Hariman's toupee. "My ex–wife Melinda and I don't much like each other and we don't want it to hurt Emily. She's a special little girl."

"I understand."

Tom Hariman winked. "You got you a girlfriend down there at the university?"

"No, sir. Not right now."

Mr. Hariman wrapped an arm around Bob's shoulder and leaned in close, confiding. "Well, let me tell you son, women sure as hell aren't as easy to understand as building design, load pressure, and shit like that. They had you read Vitruvius's *The Ten Books on Architecture* yet?"

"No, sir. Not yet," Bob said, trying to inch away. Mr. Hariman's breath smelled of mothballs.

"Well, son, the old Roman said a cube is a body with sides all of equal breadth and their surfaces perfectly square. When you throw it down, it stands firm and steady as long as you don't touch it. Just like the dice in Vegas. Now that's something you can count on."

∞ ∞ ∞

Maybe it was sleep deprivation. Bob drove past a billboard advertising Mexico, The Perfect Summer Getaway. How else could he explain it to himself—this sudden urge to take Emily, to save her from the constant moving back and forth between warring armies? Perhaps it was because he had yet to meet parents he could trust to stand firm for their children. Bob hoped there would be enough coffee brewing along the highway to keep him awake. He could feel his eyelids scraping grooves into his skull.

Five hours ago he had been in the basement of the University of Texas architecture building curled up asleep on his desk. Faith had said she was jealous of his little body. At least he could take a catnap without having to stretch out on the cold concrete floor. Bob had felt the heat come to his cheeks, but he saw she was serious. He'd had a crush on Faith since they met in the front row of a math class. The best thing was she listened to him.

"You look so cuddly when you're snoring," she'd said. Bob often found himself staring into Faith's amber–brown eyes. He was sure there was something inside them beckoning him, but he couldn't get up the nerve to ask her out. He told himself that she was too tall and that they both were busy. The pimples were building a high–rise of red splotches on Faith's pale face, like they seemed to whenever the class had a big project due. The stress was getting to all the second–year students. Their faces shone green in the fluorescent light. They haunted the basement like the living dead, backs hunched from hours spent gluing cotton–ball trees to cardboard grass.

They had less than a week to design the perfect house. Bob had tried three times to build his model. Each time he had failed.

∽ ∽ ∽

"What are you and your mom planning for your birthday, Emily?" Bob asked. They were outside Beeville and the morning was pink.

"Mommy said we can watch movies," Emily said in a sing–song. "Or we can eat ice cream. Or go to the park and play."

"That sounds fun. Is it a big park?"

Emily rubbed her fingers along the strap holding her child's car seat in place. "I don't know. I haven't been there yet. Mommy's always tired from work."

That was no surprise. Melinda Hariman had looked beat up and bone thin the two times he'd seen her—when he answered the ad, and last week when he'd first met her daughter. Bob guessed Melinda Hariman to be the kind of woman who worked hard to prove she was tough. Her lips were drawn tight when she explained the deal: $150 in cash each week and if anything happened to Emily, Bob had better plan on a short life.

"If it's not enough, I can pay more," she'd said without blinking. "It's worth it to never again have to see that son of a bitch. The court won't keep him away from Emily, but they can't force me to look at him. I'm putting my faith in you, Bob. Mr. Hariman said he wouldn't trust his daughter's life to a ditzy little co–ed. So here we are. Be extremely careful with my child."

Bob hadn't had the nerve then to ask what caused the hate to wrap around the house of Emily's parents like a python.

"Bo–Bo, Mommy says you're the schanger and you shouldn't touch me."

Emily was searching for the button on the seat belt.

Bob felt his face burning again. Even a four–year–old could make him blush. "Your mother means exchanger. She just means we're friends who drive together in a car. But you shouldn't ever let anybody touch you. Never. Okay?"

"Okay." Emily frowned. "What if we go to a store to get some candy? Can't I hold your hand?"

"Sure, Emily. Maybe we can stop soon."

Normanna, Tulita, Pawnee. The names of the towns on the passing road signs reminded Bob of being a kid and going to Catholic summer camp. Making string ties, weaving Indian bracelets, and learning the scriptures. His parents had sent him to the pseudo–wilderness every year and then left on their separate vacations. Bob remembered his father driving him to camp one year. It was just the two of them—post divorce—and the silence filled the car.

"You be good, Bobby," his father had said when they pulled up to the main building. His Dad was putting on that caring tone.

"If the bigger kids start to mess with you, stand firm. Don't show weakness. You're Daddy's boy, hear? You're capable of anything."

The words had been empty. The old man didn't know how to deal with his shrimpy son. His hopes were tied up in Mike, the younger brother, the athlete.

These days Bob hid out at school and avoided his mother's questions: "What did your father say about me this time?" He didn't dare tell her the answer was nothing. Nothing at all.

"Bo–Bo, read me a story."

Emily climbed out of the car seat and into the front seat where his architecture books were.

"Em–i–ly, what are you doing?" She reached for the car's cigarette lighter. Bob swerved the car and grabbed the lighter away from her. *You can't let your guard down for a minute.* He pulled the car into a driveway and up to Raul's Sip N Snack, a faded wooden shack with one rusty gas pump.

"That's an extreme ouchy, Emily. You can't play with it," he said and jabbed the lighter back in.

Emily looked contrite in a practiced way, her mouth pulling down at the corners. "I'm sorry. But if I had a birthday cake, I could light it."

Mustn't damage the goods in-transit, Bob said to himself and remembered Mrs. Hariman's taut lips.

"Maybe we can get you a cupcake," Bob said.

"Can I hold your hand, Bo–Bo?"

"Sure."

Bob bought a jumbo coffee and a plastic, no–spill travel mug. Emily settled on M&Ms instead of cake because she said the candies looked like little cookies.

The man behind the counter had a black eye patch.

"Well, you're sure a cute little thing," he said, taking the candy from Emily's tiny hands.

Emily climbed onto a newspaper rack and stared with her mouth open. "What's that on your eye?"

"Not now, Emily," Bob said, shrugging.

The one–eyed man's stomach jiggled as he laughed.

"That's all right. Well, I lost my eye when I was about your age. I had me a little accident is all. A pencil went through it."

Emily put her hand over her right eye. "Was it an ouchy?"

"I guess it must've been," the man said and rang the order up. His hands were huge and meaty. "But that was a long time ago. It doesn't really matter. You see, one eye's all you need. Except I can't figure distances too good. One–eighty–seven."

Bob's hands shook. He pulled two dollars from his wallet and handed the bills over.

"Can I see it?" Emily said. She stared at the eye patch.

"No, Emily. No."

The man grinned and the eye patch crinkled as his cheek rose.

"Thirteen cents change. Now, little darling, you listen to your daddy and be a good girl. I've got my eye on you."

He laughed and so did Emily. Bob managed a grin.

As they started to leave, Emily turned and said, "That's not my daddy, that's Bo–Bo."

The man squinted at Bob with his one eye. "Y'all be careful," one–eye said, scanning him, Bob imagined, as if he were memorizing the description for when he called it in to *America's Most Wanted.*

With Emily strapped securely in the child's seat, Bob aimed the car back on the highway.

"Are we there yet?" Emily asked as she ate the M&Ms.

"Not yet, Emily. We've got a ways to go."

"That's okay," she said, picking out a red M&M. "I like driving. I have two eyes."

"Emily, there's some things people don't like to talk about." He realized he was trying to explain tact to a three–year–old. "That man back there might have been sensitive."

"Mommy won't talk about some things," Emily said.

"Yeah," Bob said. "Like that."

ෆ ෆ ෆ

Karnes City was almost exactly between the Hariman's houses. Bob stopped at the Dairy Queen to use the restroom. His bladder had been aching for thirty miles from all the coffee. Emily was sleeping, so he locked the car doors.

The restaurant was crowded with teenagers, boys on one side, girls on the other, a few couples sharing booths in between. Bob wondered if they mistook him for a classmate. Faith always said he had a baby face, and his beard was light and downy like a child's hair. Faith's own pale face was probably scrunched together at this moment as she constructed her model house. Bob imagined her leaning over a drafting table, creating a roof to keep the elements at bay. Everything measured, the angles all perfect. He wished he could talk to her.

After a quick trip to the restroom, Bob noticed his stomach was growling. Since the semester began he'd gone two notches in on his belt. The excess leather drooped like a pendulum. There had been no time for food, no money until now.

"It's our voluntary concentration camp," Faith had joked a few weeks ago, red paint under her left eye. "Hitler liked to draw buildings, too, you know."

Bob ordered a hamburger and a Dr Pepper, and a little ice cream cone for Emily. He waited in the only empty booth, in the middle. Most of the Karnes City kids were wearing high school letter jackets. A boy in the corner booth punched his friend on the arm and honked with delight. Everyone was laughing. Bob stared at the back of the crew–cut red hair of another boy and the partially obscured face of the bleached blonde girl facing him.

"I couldn't believe it," the girl said. Her eyelids were painted a bright blue. "I was standing on the ledge completely naked!"

The crew cut shook. "Must've been a good party."

"Very funny, Ronny. I told you it was a dream." The blonde's eyes got wide, and she pursed her lips. "Oh, look. Isn't she precious?"

Bob turned around and Emily was standing there with her hand in her mouth. The girl was up and petting Emily's hair as if Emily were a puppy.

"Hi, baby. What is your name?"

The blonde was on her knees.

"Bo–Bo says I shouldn't talk to strangers," Emily said. Her eyes were droopy with sleep.

"Oh, I'm sorry," the blonde said, finally noticing Bob. "Your little girl is a sweetheart, Bo–Bo. Ronny and me want to have a little baby, too. Once we're married. Don't we, honey?"

Ronny stood behind her. He nodded a bucktoothed grin.

"I need to pee–pee, Bo–Bo," Emily said.

"Oh, let me take her." She stretched out a set of hot pink fingernails for Bob to shake. She couldn't be more than sixteen, he realized. "I'm Dora. There. Now we're not strangers. And I do need the practice. Don't I, Ronny?"

Crew Cut nodded again.

"Is it okay with you, Emily?" Bob asked, not relishing playing guard outside the ladies' room door.

"Can I hold her hand?"

Dora took the cue and swept Emily along. "You just don't know how precious you are, little baby."

Emily looked back at Bob and stuck out her tongue.

Bob found himself left standing with Ronny, who towered over him and shifted his weight from foot to foot.

"Where y'all from?"

"Austin," Bob answered, imagining the kid getting married in a tuxedo with a huge "KC" patch by its left lapel for Karnes City High.

"Big city. We might go on up there for our honeymoon and stay in a hotel."

He was all freckles.

"When's the wedding?" Bob wondered why a test was required to drive but not marry. He imagined Emily's parents being arrested for swerving outside the lines. Life without chance of parole.

"I dunno. After graduation, I guess."

The waitress called with Bob's order.

"Think quick, Pancek," a voice said from the corner. A French fry covered in catsup hit crew cut in the chest. The red blob stuck there. His classmates hooted as he tried to wipe it away.

"Now, y'all cut that out," Dora said, appearing from the bathroom holding Emily's hand. "Y'all quit acting like kids. My God, I'm ashamed to know you."

Emily broke free and ran to Bob. She wrapped her arms around his leg.

"We're going to eat in the car," Bob said vaguely in Crew Cut's direction and handed Emily her ice cream cone.

"I'm sorry they scared you, baby." Dora yelled from across the restaurant as they walked out. "Some people are nasty."

In the car, Emily picked up Bob's architecture book and accidentally smeared it with ice cream. "Read me a story, Bo–Bo."

She won't give up.

"Emily, this is a school book. It's a man named Frank Lloyd Wright talking about how to design a house. I don't think you'd be interested."

"Read me a story, you idiot," Emily said, louder.

Bob looked up from his hamburger. Emily was pouting.

"That's not nice, Emily. Where did you learn that word?"

"Cruella."

"Who?"

"Cruella De Ville, you idiot. She said it to Horace and Jasper when they stole the Dalmatians."

Bob realized she was talking about a cartoon.

"If you stop saying that and apologize, I'll read."

"I'm sorry, Bo–Bo."

Bob flipped through the pages looking for pictures. "I'm using this to decide what I think is the perfect house."

Emily climbed on his lap. "Read it, please."

"Okay." Bob started at the top of the page. "'What was the matter with the typical American house? Well, just for an honest beginning, it lied about everything. It had no sense of unity at all nor any such sense of space as should belong to a free people. It was stuck up in thoughtless fashion.'"

"That's silly. A house can't tell a lie unless it has a mouth. Does your house have a mouth?" Emily said.

"He doesn't mean it really lies. He means the people who design it don't think about how the house is going to be used before they build it. It's hard to explain." But easy enough to feel. Bob's memory of his parent's house was darkness. Were the shades always drawn tightly shut or was that just how he imagined it? Bob's Dad had always claimed Frank Lloyd Wright designed houses that were free like a child. But Frank Lloyd Wright himself was said to have been a lousy father.

Emily laughed. "That house is all flat on top."

"Yeah, the idea is to save money by not having a big roof and to make it fit in better with the land around it. The hard part is to keep the roof from leaking."

"I like the windows," Emily said, pointing at the full–length ones that ran along much of the house in the photo. "You can see the yard. When I'm a mommy I'll have a big yard so I can play. And a puppy. Do you have a yard, Bo–Bo?"

"No, I live in an apartment." *But I'm never there.*

He fantasized about dozing, the comforter pulled over his head. Maybe Faith in the kitchen cooking pancakes for Emily. The dog barking.

"Then you can come play in the yard at my house and walk my puppy. He won't bite you if you're nice to him," Emily said.

Through the Dairy Queen window, Bob could see Dora and Ronny at the counter. Dora waved to him, but he pretended not to notice. He imagined Ronny in an orange jumpsuit like Mr. Hariman's, Dora pelting it with catsup–covered French fries and calling Ronny a son of a bitch. He cupped his hand across his right eye, but he could still see them.

Bob handed Emily the book. "Here, you look at the pictures while I drive. Let's try to make it the rest of the way without stopping. It's getting late."

Panna Maria, Cestohowa, Kosciusko. The names were the only things exotic about these shriveling towns. The houses on the roadside were decaying.

"They look like worms," Emily said.

Bob looked at the book and saw she was right. The Wright houses were low to the ground, long and thin.

"Actually, he described them as polliwogs," Bob said, "those things that turn into frogs."

"That's funny," Emily said and laughed loud. The sound enveloped Bob like a soft blanket.

"The living area is the head and the body is the bedrooms," he said. "If a family has kids and needs more bedrooms, they just make the body longer if there is land available." *Unless its head dies.*

They were almost there. In Seguin they noticed the streets were named for birds. Bob read them to Emily one by one—Canary, Mockingbird, Hummingbird, Dove. They pretended the car had wings and Emily's mother's house was a worm below them. Bob imagined the worm wriggled out of the dirt and stared up. But it was still far away, indistinct. I need sleep, he realized.

There was a pink motel ahead. Bob considered stopping and checking in, sleeping for a day then driving again. He and Emily would live on junk food. The police would look for them, but Bob would dye his hair red, like Ronny's, and dress Emily like a boy. They would assume different lives, make up pasts, and build destinies. They would design the perfect world without parents who hire strangers to transport their children from one decaying home to the other.

In his mind, the car entered the driveway of the Amigo Motel as if on autopilot. The woman at the motel office would be wearing a

Hawaiian shirt and a sombrero. "Aloha, neighbors," she'd say, spreading her flabby arms wide. "Welcome to our humble home."

"Your hat is funny," Emily would say.

The woman would grin. Bob remembered a motel manager just like this when he was a kid and his parents took him on a disastrous cross–country vacation. The lady at the counter would say something like, "Si, Señorita. Es muy grande. We're your vacation getaway. I'm Irma. My husband Hal, the klutz, is off somewhere breaking something. Candy, little girl?" She'd reach into a plate and hand Emily a red lollipop.

"We just need the room for a while," Bob would say. "I need to rest up for our drive." *And a clean getaway.*

"Okee–dokee," Irma would say. "Local calls are free. You want some candy, big boy?"

"No. Just the room." Bob could see himself shoving two twenties out of Mrs. Hariman's generous payment across the counter.

Everything in the motel room would be pink: the carpet, the bedspread, the wallpaper, even the frame of the childlike painting above the bed of a tilting sailboat, apparently frozen in time before it was to sink.

Bob would turn on the TV to public television for Emily and drop onto the bed. The sound would be up too high, but he wouldn't have the energy to get up and turn it down. Emily would cross her legs on the floor, stare into the TV's greenish glow and smile as Barney the purple dinosaur started loudly, "I love you, you love..."

Bob remembered reading about some parent who formed the I Hate Barney Club. On the same page was a story about three boys who assaulted a guy in a Barney costume at a Kmart. They were too old, one step from being teenagers. Emily would be under Barney's spell. There was hope.

The room would be cold, so Bob would nestle his hand in his pants pocket. He'd finger a piece of paper and pull it out. On it would be written "M. Hariman" and a number. He'd reach for the telephone and start dialing. The receiver would rub at his ear. He'd hear it ring twice. Hang up, he'd tell himself, but wouldn't. He couldn't.

"He–llo," Melinda Hariman would say in a sing–song voice like Emily's.

Bob imagined her in her apartment, cleaning it, arranging the toys for Emily.

"Hello?"

Barney on the TV again. The song's other version: "I hate you, you hate me…"

"Is someone there?"

The words would come out of Bob's mouth, but they'd seem disconnected from him, distant.

"It's Robert, uh, Bob, Mrs. Hariman."

"My god, Bob, you had me scared for a minute." She'd sound relieved, but fear would seep in. "Is Emily okay? Oh, please don't tell me something's happened to my baby."

Bob would look over at Emily, her head bobbing to Barney's song. "She's fine. She's watching Barney."

"Barney? Where are you? I told you I don't want unnecessary stops." She'd pause. "I thought you understood."

Bob imagined his eyes closing tightly as he pushed his head into the bedspread. It would scratch at his neck. "I'm sorry," he'd whisper into the phone, his face tight. "We're not coming back."

He felt Emily's hand on his arm. "Do you have any magic books?" she asked.

Bob turned and saw Emily's smiling face. In his mind he banged down the telephone receiver. The motel was already a mile behind them.

Emily frowned.

"I need a magic book."

Bob felt a row of sweat droplets seep from his upper lip. What was he thinking? Then Bob started laughing. He tried to stifle it, but he couldn't, like he couldn't when he was a kid on one of the family's rare trips to church. But this time his mother wasn't here turning red with anger.

"What's so funny, Bo–Bo?" Emily asked and started giggling.

"Nothing, Emily. Nothing at all. I'm sorry, what was that about magic?"

"If we had a magic book, then I could cast a spell and my Mommy and Daddy could both be at my birthday party."

"I'm fresh out of magic," Bob said.

They sailed quietly through the town of Geronimo. If he'd pulled into that motel, the police would soon have been looking for the car. His name would be in the newspapers. I just want to make a safe place for Emily, he'd say if they ever found them. It would make the headlines nationwide. But they wouldn't understand; they'd get it wrong.

"Let's play a game, Emily," Bob said. "Pretend I'm your mommy and daddy for a while. Okay?"

"That's silly," Emily said. "You can't be Mommy and Daddy."

"It's just a game," Bob said, forcing a grin.

"Okay, but I get allowance," Emily said, "and toys."

"You got it, Fred. That's your new name. I forgot to tell you, you're a little boy now."

Emily pursed her lips. "Then I get a car."

"Okay."

Settled. Bob's mind was racing. Everything would be perfect. Just me and my boy Fred. But something was missing. Faith. He forgot about Faith.

Bob spotted a telephone at the Sac N Pac on the edge of San Marcos and pulled in. A little girl and her mother had set up a card table and were selling Girl Scout cookies.

The call was picked up after six rings. "You've reached Hell. What the hell do you want?" Bob recognized the voice. Bertelson from design class. He sounded delirious.

"It's Bob. Get Faith for me."

"Yes'm, Mister Bob. Anything for you, Mister Bob."

Bob reached into his wallet, pulled out two dollars, and waved it at the Girl Scout. She brought him a box of each type of cookie. He leaned down and took the chocolate mints.

"Bob, is that you?" Faith sounded surprisingly awake.

"Yeah, it's me."

"Guess what? I finished my house," she said. "It's perfect!"

Bob watched Emily climb into the driver's seat and play with the steering wheel.

"That's great, Faith. Listen I've got a surprise for you. Okay if I come by and pick you up?"

Emily honked the horn twice.

"I guess. Where are you?"

"On my way home," he said and shook a finger at Emily.

"It's none of my business, but shouldn't you be working on your house, too?" Faith's voice was light like marshmallows.

A scratchy laugh forced its way up from deep in Bob's throat. "As a matter of fact, I'm working on it right now. I'll show you when I get there."

Bob hung up and went to the passenger door. He buckled Emily firmly in place. She rested her feet on top of his architecture books.

"Excuse me, Fred," Bob said. "Have some cookies." He handed Emily the box and moved her feet aside. The books made a teetering pile in his arms. Bob could feel the sweat dripping down his sides as he struggled with the weight.

"No magic," Emily said to him in a half question, half statement.

He poured the books onto the card table in front of the Girl Scout's mother as if it were an offering to the gods of the happy family. Maybe they could find the right home, the one that eluded him.

"Here," Bob said. "You might like these."

The woman shrugged her shoulders and backed away from him.

"Thanks, I guess," she said.

Her arm was stretched taut in the air next to her, a wall in front of her daughter, as he walked away.

Emily's face was smeared with chocolate. Bob wiped his sleeve across her lips and got most of it.

"It's my turn to drive, Bo–Bo," Emily said when they were back on the highway.

"That would be nice, Fred. But I don't think you can reach the pedals."

"Yes, I can," Emily said, taking hold of an imaginary steering wheel. "See? Now I'm the mommy and you're the baby."

"Are we there yet?" Bob asked and laughed.

"Dear, I told you we'll be there soon," Emily said, her forehead wrinkling. "Now be still or you won't get any cookies."

Bob stared out at the highway and imagined being three-years old. His mother used to put him to sleep with this nonsense song, "Pumpkin–pumpkin–pumpkin …" The sound of her voice made his eyes droop.

"Sit still, dear," Emily said. "You'll make mommy have a crick."

He was sure she meant wreck, but Bob didn't correct her. The steering wheel felt huge in his hands.

"What's for dinner, Mommy?" Bob asked. It was like he ate that hamburger in another lifetime.

"Ice cream and cake and spinach," Emily said. Her voice was monotone. "And if you're a good baby, you can have cookies."

"When do we eat?" Bob asked. He liked spinach.

"Dear, mommy has to work so we're going to stop and get chicken instead. Here it is." Emily handed Bob an invisible box.

"But I want spinach," Bob said. He saw an Austin City Limit sign pass. They were ten minutes from home, his with Faith in the school basement or Mrs. Hariman's. He couldn't decide. *Olly olly all come free.*

"Dear, if you don't eat your food, you can't have dessert."

"What's daddy going to eat?" Bob said without thinking, mentally retrieving the words from his mouth.

"Daddy can't eat, dear," Emily said and stared sternly ahead. "He's working. He's working on the railroad and growing weeds. Eat your dinner." ల

THE SCREENWRITER

THE VIOLINIST IS BACK at it, playing soft background music, and Mary sways with the notes. Bob has rejoined his father and I am leaning on the nurse's station counter wondering what to do next, feeling like a vulture waiting to feast on grief.

The woman in the wheelchair is smiling and I notice all of the candies are gone from her tray. Like in an old *Star Trek* episode, she is operating on a different time frequency than the rest of us. We whirr past like insects while she contemplates in chocolate time.

Mary walks over to the man in the bed and presses the control to raise his head so he can get a better view of the musician.

"How's that work for you, Mr. Belacek?"

He mouths "fine" but no sound comes out. I can see the words pooling inside him.

Mary returns to the counter and whispers to me, "Talk to him."

I know nothing about the man, so I slip down to the volunteer office and check the book.

I remember Annie May's instructions: "These are our cheat sheets. The book is always here on the desk. Check it first thing when you come in. It'll tell you who our latest residents are, what ails them, and maybe a little about who they are."

Alfred Belacek. A Dallas attorney born and raised in Vermont. Prep schools. A dead wife. No children.

Mr. Belacek's eyes follow me as I come back down the hallway. I lean over close to him.

"I picked blueberries once in Vermont," I say. "You must have had an exciting life as an attorney, too."

His eyes are a crystal blue. He purses his lips, massaging the words, and motions for me to come even closer. I lean my ear toward his face, and he spits the words loose like chunks of gravel.

"Pole vault champion."

His blue eyes train on mine and I can see into his past for a moment. The young, nimble boy grabbing the pole. Running. Taking flight.

Mr. Belacek's mouth curls into a satisfied grin and his eyes drift shut. The effort to speak seems to have drained his battery.

"What'd he say?" Mary asks from the nurse's station.

When I tell her, she puts her palm on my forehead.

"You've got the power," she says. "You got more out of him in five minutes than I have in days. I am impressed."

Mary points to a high shelf where stuffed animals are lined up, their legs dangling down.

"My favorite patient had her daughter buy those. One a day. They were her lucky charm. Her bed was crowded with them in the end. Said it was only fitting—she was dying in a zoo, so might as well make it official. I've got her giraffe at home."

"How do you handle this job?" I ask.

Mary turned her back to me.

"Her name was Mona. I hid in the back room and cried the day she left." She turns to me, the sadness clouding her face. "I don't always do that. Lots of faces blend together. It's like at a party where you're drawn to some people more than others. Some patients are obnoxious or boring. But I went to Mona's funeral. And I cried some more. Then I read her obituary in the newspaper and cried again."

"How did she handle dying?" I ask. That's the real mystery I want answered: what it feels like to die. The cold hard facts.

"As serene as an infant taking a nap," Mary says, and puts her hand on mine. "They're not all like that."

She grips my hand tightly.

"One man grabbed me just like that, maybe harder. It was about twenty minutes before he passed."

"He was afraid?" I ask.

Her touch lightens.

"Pure fear," she says. "It was even worse after he was gone. One time my granny's cat died. I found Lil Bit on the bed with her mouth and eyes open wide. He looked like that kitty. He didn't want to go."

At that moment, with her guard down, Mary is the most beautiful woman in the world. The wrinkles, the years fall from her face. Unlike most of the people I meet in this world, she's being honest and nothing could be sexier. I long to take her in my arms and cradle her, but I don't. I just ask more questions.

"How do the other nurses handle it?"

She takes one step backward and the businesslike nurse wall goes back up.

"Different ways, Matt." She turns and jots a note on a patient's chart. "Some throw pebbles in a pond. Others burn candles. We've got a few praying types. Ritualistic crap like that. Whatever works. If you're a nurse here, you've got to grieve."

I look back at the dozing Mr. Belacek and the woman caught in chocolate time. I try to comprehend that they'll likely be dead in the next couple of days. The vulture watches.

"What else do nurses have to do, Mary?"

She holds up three fingers and counts them off.

"First off, you've got to have boundaries. Then you've got be ready for the busy and the slow times. Thank the lord for a high vacancy rate; our souls need that break now and then. And you've got to know the truth when you see it."

"That's it?"

"Isn't that enough? Oh, and it's super important to recognize when you're burned out. My boy Jason is getting close to college age so I'd better not burn out too quickly. Besides, I'm used to our main clientele, the elderly. Been around the old buzzards for years, and I'm getting a bit long in the tooth myself." ℘

THE FEMALE NURSE

I'M CONVINCED THAT WAS the day I became old.

I had dipped my feet into the lukewarm water and settled down at the edge of the pool to watch Jason swim. I brought along a paperback copy of *Out of Africa* with every intention of reading up for this class I was taking one night a week in the adult education department over at the college.

My husband Gary looked at me kind of funny when I mentioned going to school. Gary was an assistant pressman and most days he came home covered with ink from head to toe. Sometimes I made him strip before I would even allow him in the apartment door. To hell with what our neighbors thought; there was no turning back when that ink set in on a rug or upholstery. And I believe that whole thing kept the spark in our marriage. Those black hands would start grabbing me while that snow–white belly followed along to watch. The carpets and upholstery may have been safe, but we sure ruined some sheets. It should have come as no surprise. Gary was as predictable as a situation comedy, particularly when it came to being horny.

But sometimes Gary did surprise me. Like when I told him the class was $50 for six weeks and he didn't complain one bit. Looking back, I imagined he liked the idea of having some time to himself. Of course, he was never too alone with Jason bouncing off the walls and asking those weird questions. "What are trees made of? Why? Do you have to make the food hot? Why? Can I be a mommy? Why not?" When they're tiny, it's a game to get them to say a word. Later on that game can come back to haunt you.

Jason called the swimming pool his jellybean because of the way it was shaped. He always said, "I want to jump in my jellybean!" It may sound silly now, but it was cute coming from a four–year–old going on five.

Big, gray clouds floated across the sky and threatened to rain the last bit of summertime away. But mostly it was sunny. The TV weatherman said the temperature would drop almost 20 degrees that night and fall would have fallen.

That's why Jason and I were getting our last swim of the year in at the Stardust Apartments. I suspected it might be the last swim, period, at the Stardust, since we were the only family to come near the pool. The private grade school next door went and bought up the whole complex. The fund drive was on and whenever the millions were piled up in the bank, the Stardust would be gobbled up and a new gymnasium born to take its place. The school folks already had taken to boarding up the windows of any apartment that went vacant. It was as if the building was dying by sections. And forget about getting any major repairs done. They flat wouldn't spend the money. If Mr. Thompson, the apartment manager for the past twenty-four years, couldn't find a way to fix it, it likely would stay broke. Gary always said Mr. Thompson was as old as God and twice as skinny. But Mr. Thompson was a youngster compared to some of our neighbors. Otis Ringer was my favorite. He invented a particular variety of pinto beans. He sold the recipe to one of those big food companies fifteen, maybe twenty years before, but they still let him visit the plant once a year and act like the boss. Most afternoons he stood in front of the apartment complex acting like he was late for an important meeting. He stood there, swaying slightly on the balls of his feet and looking expectantly down the road. Mr. Ringer's clothing was old and tattered and his shirt was splattered with samples of past meals. Pathetic, but he was quite the flirt. He'd get this big smile whenever he saw me coming and he was always giving me free cans of those beans.

"Sweet legumes for the sweet lady," Mr. Ringer would say and stiffly bow. Those beans gave Gary the worst kind of gas.

Yeah, living at the Stardust was like being in Never–Never Land. By simple comparison to the other tenants it was hard for us to feel the days drip away into years. That was one faucet leak that the landlord couldn't fix.

ഗ ഗ ഗ

I couldn't keep Jason in those water wings for the life of me. He was surely part fish. He patrolled the bottom of the pool looking for a nickel or a dime that maybe fell out of somebody's swim trunks. Once he gathered fifty cents and paid for his own Coke out of the machine they had next to the apartment's washing machines. I suspect Jason will be a banker one day.

Jason was over by where the diving board used to be when this noise started drifting across from the other side of the fence. He was writing his name in the grime that had collected on the blue tiles right atop the water line. The diving board was leaning against the faded bricks of the apartment complex. I guess the school officials assumed their insurance wouldn't cover damaged spinal cords at their new property. I didn't argue. Jason was too young to be on that diving board.

Anyway, the noises Jason and I heard were playful and organized—the whooping sounds that are somewhere between a boo and a bark repeated over and over. Like audiences on talk shows used to do when things got wild.

I guess the wooden privacy fence around the Stardust's pool was brown once, but by then it tended toward sun–bleached white and maybe gray. The gaps between the individual planks varied from next to nothing to about a half an inch. The tops of the boards sloped up and slid down like the tracks on a roller coaster. Over by the gate were a couple of signs Mr. Thompson had nailed up. They were stark white with black lettering spelling out NO GLASS CONTAINERS and NO SWIMMING AFTER 10 PM, except the NOs on both of them were done in red.

After the whooping died down, somebody switched on a stereo and fast–talking rap music blared out. I could see through the gaps in the fence this row of bright white T–shirts line up and start quivering and jumping around to the beat. Jason swam over to the swimming pool ladder and clung to it while he watched. When the song was over those white T–shirts started whooping again, this time with some little–girl laughter and clapping thrown in.

Those little T–shirts couldn't sit still. All I could see was their backsides, but it was clear the little bodies inside the shirts were wiggling around and moving their little feet.

"OK, girls," this megaphone voice said. "Line up and give me your undivided attention."

I could just start to make out their heads. All but one had shiny blond hair, with the other one a redhead. One of the blond girls shook her hair down in her face and, with a jerk, whipped it back over her head where it bounced into place. I tried to wiggle mine in imitation, but ended up with frizzled hair sticking to my teeth.

"Let's get it right this time, girls," the megaphone woman said.

One of the dark clouds floated over the sun, making the shadows disappear. I remember the summer prior to that one Mr. Thompson got a hummingbird feeder and filled it with colored sugar water. There was this big oak tree that hung out over the swimming pool and made Mr. Thompson's life miserable with more leaves scattering across the water right when he was finished cleaning another batch out. He hung that hummingbird feeder in the oak where the tree started to curve. Mr. Thompson thought he was being sly putting it out there on a thin wire so the squirrels couldn't get to it. But those squirrels were tricky. I'd sit for hours watching while Jason swam. A hummer would flap its wings to beat the band about ten feet off from the tree, watching along with me. This squirrel would climb the tree and half jump, half stretch until his two back feet rested on the tree and his two front paws were on the feeder. It was a shaky situation, but he sucked that sugar water down like he had rediscovered his squirrel mother's tit.

The first time I saw that squirrel do his act, I chased him away and let that hummingbird fly up and drink its fill. But then I got to thinking the squirrel would probably climb right back up once I went inside. Some things you can't change no matter how hard you try. I suppose it comes down to survival of the fittest or most acrobatic as the case may be. Next time I sat and watched the squirrel slurp on the sugar water I felt fine.

I was like that squirrel when I was in school. "Always rooting around in what doesn't concern you," my mother would say. We studied Africa in fifth grade and I wanted to be an explorer; my cousin Pitt had his tonsils out and I wanted to be a doctor. These days I watched Jason explore and I read books, but I didn't want to be a writer. They hid away from life too much. My dream was always to be up front where people could see me living. Like that furry creature dangling in the tree.

Mr. Thompson didn't care much for that squirrel. He complained about always having to fill that "damn feeder," as he called it. He said sugar water didn't grow on trees. I didn't presume to tell him a sugar cane looked suspiciously like a tree in my opinion. Mr. Thompson tried everything he could to beat that squirrel. He went so far as to slather Crisco shortening all over that tree. He used a paintbrush and made a real mess. We learned one thing: ants love Crisco. The squirrel used those ants as a footstool. He smooshed a bunch when he walked across.

But this year Mr. Thompson brought out the hummingbird feeder again. At first, he said damned if he was going to add a touch of class to the Stardust if the owners were willing to let the apartment complex go to hell in a hand basket. He said it, not me. The thing to keep in mind is the school next door that owned the apartments was one of those private religious outfits named after some saint. I didn't feel too comfortable talking about a saint going to hell. I know people who might even call that sacrilegious. But Mr. Thompson kept trying to outsmart that squirrel.

I could see the white T–shirts start to shake around again on the other side of the fence. "WE–ARE–BLUE–AND–WHITE. WILDCATS–FIGHT–FIGHT–FIGHT," they yelled, pointing their arms in the air, then bowing them out by placing their hands on their hips. I knew screaming and clapping wasn't far away. I suppose we were all young once. Sometimes it's hard for me to remember; other times it burns inside my chest. I looked at Jason romping in the water and I saw myself almost twenty–five years before, doing the exact same thing. Competing with my brother Donny to see who could hold an underwater handstand the longest without tipping over. Or shouting, "Marco ... Polo ... Marco ..." while Donny kept his eyes shut tight and wildly reached out his hands for me. Our fingers and toes wrinkled like the cheeks of old people, but Donny and I didn't care as long as we could swim a few minutes longer.

Tiny raindrops started to dent the water around my feet and pushed the memories away. I reached down, got a handful of swimming pool water and splattered it on my face, which was feeling flushed from the sun despite the clouds hovering.

I remembered how my mother always said it's dangerous to swim when rain is falling and yelled at Jason to get out of the pool. Jason dove straight to the bottom, pretending he didn't hear a word. I eased into the pool until the water reached the bottom of my nose and pretended I was an elephant cooling her snout at an oasis.

The water looked green, probably because the pool hadn't seen paint on its bottom in a number of years. Mr. Thompson believed chemicals were the only solution to swimming pool problems. He spent more on chlorine than he even did on Crisco. I could see white flecks float in the pool water like the tiny snowflakes in one of those water–filled things you shake up to bring winter down on a little plastic village.

Gary had been saying we needed to start looking for a new place to live. We knew it wouldn't be easy finding a place that cheap, especially one with all bills paid. Gary said you can't hardly find that kind of deal these days. He didn't care much for the idea of me going back to work. He said it wasn't worth the cost of day care. In my opinion it was looking like a necessity.

We'd lived in the Stardust since I got out of the hospital after Jason was so kind as to abandon the womb. Jason and I were both looking a little ragged at that point. Gary drove us up to the Stardust and said, "Welcome home." We'd been living in my mother's spare bedroom up till then. I was shocked, but I couldn't stop smiling. Gary walked me through the doorway of Apartment 110 while I held Jason tight to my chest. My little baby sure has grown since then. We laughed then about how old our neighbors were, but to ourselves. They were nice people, always wanting to talk. They made us feel so young.

The rain started coming down in huge drops. The white T–shirts screamed and ran for cover. I waited for Jason to come up for air. He flew out of the water like he had springs on his feet, then sank back in up to his neck. I told Jason again that it was time to go, this time giving him the stare that said I meant it.

"Ah, mom," he said, rolling his eyes and splashing water in my direction. "I'm a fish. I have to stay in water."

"Now, Jason," I told him.

The rain was really coming down. Besides, I had to get dressed for my class and find some time to read a little of that book. The night before I'd told Gary it felt good, even if it wasn't exactly a real college class. He smiled and gave me a squeeze, but I don't know if he understood.

Gary was on the couch in all his inky glory staring at the blank TV screen when Jason and I came in the apartment door wrapped in beach towels. I admit seeing that ink touching my couch ticked me off, but I knew an argument would just make me madder and probably end with me being late for class. I brought Jason into the bathroom, stripped him down, and toweled his hair dry. He hopped off to his bedroom in search of his Ninja Turtle pajamas while I applied some blush to my cheeks.

Gary lit up a cigarette when I wandered back into the living room looking for my purse. His eyes focused on me for a second and then he looked away. I asked him if something was the matter and he studied his fingertips for the answer. He smashed his cigarette out like it was a bug.

"They told us today that they're going to have to cut back some at work. Times are hard, they said. Some of us have to go. I think I'm one of them. Honey, I don't mind telling you I'm scared. I don't see how we can get us another apartment if I don't have a job."

Something in the way he said it made my legs shake. I climbed on Gary's lap and wrapped an arm around his neck, leaning my cheek on the warmth of his.

"Gary, we'll get by somehow. You'll find another job, or we can always move in with my mother until things settle down. Besides, it's not like they're kicking us out of this place tomorrow. They aren't sure when they'll be ready to tear it down. And I can always get a job, too, you know."

He stiffened after that last part. "You didn't check the mail today, did you, honey?"

I shrugged my shoulders and shook my head. "I guess we were too busy swimming. Why?"

"There's a legal thing posted over the mailboxes. I don't speak lawyer too well, but I read it to say we've got a month to get out. If we clean up, it says they'll give us our full deposit back."

"But Mr. Thompson would have told us."

"You'd think so," Gary said. He pulled back from me, crossed his arms tight at his chest and pruned his lips up in thought. He always does that lip thing when he's nervous. "I guess maybe Thompson didn't know anything about it until today either. Least that's all I can figure."

I could see Gary was really scared, but right then I had this very real urge to bolt out the door and never look back. Just keep running and running. Maybe go to the jungle and consult with a witch doctor.

I traced my fingers gently over Gary's hair, kissed him on the cheek, and said not to worry. We could talk about it later. I told him I was late for class, grabbed my books, and went out that door.

The funny thing was I didn't go to class. I started to walk to the Pinto, but for some reason I ended up out by the swimming pool. Over the fence and through a lighted window I could see a janitor bending to clean a classroom in the empty school. The chairs were upside down, resting on the tiny desks until the morning. I looked by the tree, but the squirrel was nowhere to be found. The empty hummingbird feeder swayed in the breeze. The rain was down to a fine mist. I sat on a wet lounge chair and let moisture collect in dots on my hair. After a while the sky faded to dark, but the clouds cleared and the stars came out in droves. A thousand little sparks lit up the sky and I felt lost in them. All that dampness was giving me the chills. I went and sat on the lawn next to the pool. I took my shoes off and dug up clumps of grass with my toes.

Words kept repeating in my head. I must have heard them a million times way back in high school. We stood in the bleachers admiring the football players' butts. Spiking the Cokes we drank out of wax cups with shots of whiskey from flasks we smuggled in zipped–up in our purses. The cheerleaders on the edge of the track in their bright white uniforms repeating: "WE'VE–GOT–SPIRIT, YES–WE–DO. WE'VE–GOT–SPIRIT, HOW–'BOUT–YOU?"

We bundled up in our prettiest sweaters and fanciest coats to keep warm on football nights. That night at the Stardust, the cool breeze pushed the cloudy water against the sides of the pool again and again, sending chlorine perfume my way.

I don't know what came over me. I stood up fast in the wet grass, just as quickly dropped, and spread my legs as far as I could into what we used to call the splits. My arms stretched straight out at my sides. I stared up at the endless pool of stars and let loose with a whoop. Then another. I pulled my hands in and started clapping real loud. I couldn't seem to stop. ☙

THE SCREENWRITER

WHEN I RETURN SATURDAY morning, I find myself afraid to go inside the hospice. I park out back and loiter in the car drinking the last of my coffee. I was up late trying to figure this out. What am I accomplishing? I don't even have a title, much less a screenplay. What I have are a bunch of nuggets. I need a story. I need some structure. I need a plot point to pump up the action on page thirty. All I'm getting is more angry at death, the subject no one in the real world will talk about. Like the rest, I've spent most of my life avoiding the subject, feeling invincible.

I lock the car and stare at the back fence. The true reason I'm scared to go inside is that when I do a few more people will have died. As long as I linger, there's a flicker of hope for them.

The back patio is the product of one of those fund–raising projects where people buy a brick in honor of a loved one. I shove my hands in my pockets and float around reading the inscriptions. Some are generic: "Rest in Peace," "Our Beloved Mother," "We'll Miss You." Others have a creative flair: "A Bluebonnet in God's Halo," "Buena Suerte, Lil Bro."

From inside the glass of the door, I spot the back of a head and I recognize it as Bob. Mr. Wright is alive. The knowledge is enough to finally propel me inward.

Bob is facing away from me on one of the couches. His feet are up on a coffee table and he's reading one book with another in his lap. I recognize the unread one as the Bible from the other day.

I start to think about him as a potential character. A character needs a worldview to operate from. Is Bob's a religious one? A character also must have a dramatic need. Bob's has got to somehow have to do with his relationship with his father. A need to prove himself to the old man? Most of all a prominent character needs to undergo some sort of change. Nothing big required. We take baby steps in life.

Bob turns in profile toward me and grins.

"Hey, buddy. We've been wondering where you were."

I make out the book's title: *Understanding Death*, and walk over.

"Day job has kept me busy."

"Anything fun?"

"Just pays the bills. Not worth mentioning."

I sit in the chair across from him and look for the details. Unshaven. Barefoot with socks. T–shirt and jeans. These are vacation clothes.

"I'm settling in," Bob says as if reading my thoughts. He speaks slowly, as if he, like his father, must search for the words. "It's great to come out in the middle of the night and talk to the nurses."

"Your father OK?"

"Asleep. He's turned into a vampire. Sleeps most of the day and stays up all night." Bob points to the book on dying. "It's all in here. Part of the process."

"Is the Bible helping?"

"I thought I'd give it a try," Bob says and fingers the leather cover. "Not really my family's style. We're a bunch of heathens. Faith is a prickly pear. You know what the weirdest thing is?"

"I couldn't guess."

"Knowing life will go on without Dad." He points toward the door. "A little while ago an ice cream truck came down the road. I automatically started searching my pockets for change, like I was twelve. A little death can't stop the ice cream man."

"What flavor?"

"I craved a strawberry bar, the kind with bits of crust sprinkled on. I chickened out. Didn't seem right. Though I bet Dad would appreciate it."

"He's a cool guy."

"Yeah. Thanks."

"No problem."

Inside I'm throwing jealous daggers at Bob, wishing I could have had half the relationship with my father that he appears to have with his.

"No, I mean he said you made him face facts. Two nights ago, about four in the morning, Dad told me he couldn't breathe. He was sweating a lot, and his fingers started to turn blue." Bob holds out his hand and stretches his fingers between us.

I nod and see a major plot point of my screenplay materialize.

"Up until then, I still thought he'd go home," Bob says. "We still have the Christmas tree up from before he went into the hospital. Keep waiting to open the presents. It's a fire hazard by now."

"But he's OK now?"

"It's like he caught a second wind. He started ordering me and my sister around. Told us to get ready. Marching orders is what he called it."

Bob's foot slips off the coffee table, and he sits up.

"Last night the relatives gathered around his bed. We opened a whiskey bottle and told stories. Dad was in and out, but it was a moment. It was truly a moment."

I search his eyes for sadness and can't find a trace.

"Did you know about the baby?" Bob says.

I shake my head no.

"They moved her in yesterday. Born with brain damage. I've seen the parents in passing. A couple in their twenties."

Bob puts the book down.

"My uncle was here and he whispered something in my ear. He said you're officially a man when your father dies."

"Somebody told me that at my dad's funeral," I say. "I don't know if I buy it. You?"

Bob blinks at me. "I'll let you know soon."

∽ ∽ ∽

I go into the volunteer office to check the book and think of what Annie May told me that first day about being a volunteer: Give the hospice patients what they want—this isn't a hospital. Make them comfortable. Go away when they tell you to. Ask questions. Listen. Wear your nametag at all times.

The chocolate candy lady has died, so have Mr. Belacek and a few others I never got to meet. Lots of new people, mostly women, mostly elderly. The baby's name is Shawn. He's two weeks old and visitors are strictly forbidden.

I look up and Annie May's presence fills the room.

"Matt! I heard you were poking around," she says. "You find that story yet? People need somebody to tell them to. That's why you're allowed here. That's why I'm here. Somebody's got to take it all in before they fly away. They need that."

"I think I'm getting close," I say.

"Well, alright then." She puts her hand on my shoulder and leans in closer. "It's time I told you mine. You up for it?"

I nod, and she sits down across from me.

"My husband died two years ago in Room Seven. Husband number three. We had him in the hospice the last couple of days. Most folks aren't here more than a week before they pass. There's exceptions, but that's the rule."

"Like Mr. Wright," I say.

"Yeah. You like him, don't you? Me, too. He's got the spirit."

Annie May looks me in the eyes, and I can tell I've passed her trust test.

"Now, about my husband? The folks here treated him like he was important. He was a working man, and they treated him like he mattered. That's why I'm here every weekend. But I like it here, too. I like the way this place swirls around me like a pretty silk ribbon. I like how nobody asks me how I'm doing or talks about the weather. That's my short version. Now what's your story?"

"I told you. . . ."

"A screenplay. Right. I respect that."

A serious–faced young black man appears behind her and grips Annie May's shoulder. She yanks at the hand.

"Want you to meet my son Anthony," she says. "He's a college boy. Making his Mama proud."

Anthony nods toward me.

"What are you studying?" I ask.

"Business," he says.

"Matt is making a movie," Annie May says. "Maybe one day you can be his money man."

"I got to get through math first," he says. "You trying to figure out the dying folk?"

"Yeah," I say. "Haven't figured out much yet."

Annie May squeezes Anthony's hand more tightly.

"I tried to shield Anthony and my youngest boy James from death," Annie May says. "Don't know why. Nobody's going to escape it. But I got their behinds to church regular."

Anthony grins, and for a second he looks like a young boy.

"We found out a lot when she weren't looking," he says and winks at me. ☙

THE STUDENT

MAMA SAID, DON'T YOU go over there, don't you even think about it.

We was watching it all on TV. There must have been seven fire trucks in all. Hoses was unwrapped. Water was flying everywhere. The white lady on TV said it was a total loss. It was cool. We could hear the sirens going from outside and on the TV at the same time. You could tell there was a big crowd of people watching the flames. It smelled smoky.

I could hardly sleep all night. Neither could James. He kept peeking out the window. James is a little Mama's boy and he never seen a fire before. I never seen one that big and I'm thirteen.

Mama never would let us go down there. They opened last month, the TV lady said. We seen them building it for about a week before that.

"Oddities of the World." That's what the big sign out front said. It was two big wooden buildings out in a field off the highway is all. It used to be a flea market and Mama took us there to buy some clothes one time. All I remember is this guy selling about a hundred different kinds of sunglasses.

But that was before these men came along and painted the place red, white, and blue. Mama said all it is now is a bar with two–headed chickens and three–legged goats running around doing their business on everybody's shoes.

I said I never seen no two–headed chicken, what's it look like? She said you ain't never going to see one neither. She said it would look like dinner if she got her hands on it.

James and me got up early and fixed ourselves Cheerios. We poured the milk over the top even though you could tell by smelling it the milk was going funny. Mama works Saturdays. They like any other day, she says. Except Sunday. Sometimes on Sunday we go to church and sometimes Mama says she has to rest up a bit.

But this was only Saturday and Mama said, Anthony, you watch out for your little brother now; he's only five and you can't be leaving him to run off causing trouble with those friends of yours. James said he'll be six next month. Mama squinted her eyes at him and smiled. Yes you will, she said, and we'll have us a nice party.

You keep him in one piece until then, she said, pointing them eyes at me. Don't you go over there. You hear me?

Yes, ma'am, I told her, my eyes glued on the TV. James said he won't go neither. The screen door popped shut and we listened to the engine rev a while before the car backed out and faded away.

Claude didn't bother to knock, just stuck his big head in the door and asked if I seen it. James said he seen it. Claude said shut up, squirt, and sat down on the couch to watch TV. We watched superhero cartoons. James likes them.

Claude said he wondered what started it anyway. Said it sure did burn pretty. He asked if I seen it.

I seen it, I seen it, I told him.

We watched it on the TV, James said.

Watch your cartoons and be quiet, I said to James. I told Claude I'd like to know what happened to all them animals. Maybe they burned.

Claude laughed. What animals? he asked.

They got two–headed boats, James said.

He means goats, I said, rolling my eyes.

Claude shook his head back and forth and smiled. Man, you don't know nothing, do you? He put his hands behind his head and sunk down into the couch.

Claude always thinks he knows everything. Mr. Cool, that's him. He sat waiting for me to ask. But I wouldn't do it. I would not ask. This superhero guy was taking a bomb to outer space to explode it and save everybody. I kept my eyes on the TV and let Claude wait.

Claude pulled out a cigarette and asked me for a light. James started jumping up and down and screaming, I'm gonna tell! I'm gonna tell! James won't keep nothing a secret from Mama unless I give him something, even then he usually ends up telling on me anyway. But I ain't afraid to get in trouble. James is a little kid, and little kids are that way—they got nothing to hide yet.

I fished some matches out from underneath the couch. I keep all kinds of stuff under the couch. Magazines, letters, the ads for bras out of Mama's newspapers, a few packs of cigarettes. It's all safe there as long as Mama don't go crazy and start cleaning everything. And I got to make sure James don't see and tell on me. He heard the preacher say that little boys don't start growing into sinning men until they learn to keep secrets from their Mamas and Papas. The little Mama's boy been a holy pain ever since.

James finally got tired of acting like a retard and sat back down all big–eyed. Claude grinned and grabbed the matchbook from me. He opened it with one hand, bent a match down, and flicked it across the black strip. He held it up in James' face when the tip started to glow.

Just like that, he said, lighting his cigarette off the flame. It went up just like that.

James' eyes got even bigger, if that's possible, and his mouth hung open.

Animals weren't no problem; they didn't burn none, Claude said, shaking the flame out with a turn of his wrist. They was a front. My cousin Ralph told me what really goes on over there.

Yeah, I know, drinking, I said, trying to look bored and worldly.

Drinking and women, Claude said. Women you can buy.

Yuck, James said, I wouldn't spend my money on no girls.

Shut up, James, I said. You ain't got no money, so you don't need to be worrying about it, now do you?

Mama said don't go over there, James said, pushing his hands in at his sides and puffing his lips out like they was the beak on a chicken. A chicken with only one head.

You tell her and you be dead, I said, grabbing a cigarette from Claude. You stay here and watch cartoons and keep that tongue in your mouth.

James set his jaw and said he was gonna see it.

Listen, boy, Claude said, you stick with the TV, leave the living to men like your brother Anthony and me. There's things there you'd never recover from. We'd be spoon feeding you and changing your diapers every hour. No, sir, some things boys wasn't meant to see.

James shifted from foot to foot and wiped his nose. I get to go or I'm gonna tell Mama, he said, looking hard at Claude.

I shook my head. We better let him come, I said. We ain't got time to argue about it. Mama'll be home for dinner in a few hours. You don't get out of my sight. Hear me, James?

Claude grabbed James by the head and sniffed at him. I smell fear, he said. Yep, there's no mistaking that powerful odor. Like when a skunk gets crushed by a car on the highway. It never comes off.

Leave him alone, I said, grabbing James and pushing him out the door.

You got to walk across a big field to get there. The grass was grown almost over James' head. He had to walk tiptoe to see anything. Just a head bobbing across the tops of the grass.

But he knew we were getting close. Clown food. That's what James said.

Claude pruned his face up and said, Huh? What's he talking about now? You ain't supposed to go crazy till after you seen what's in store for you, boy.

He's talking about that smell, I said. Ever since Mama took us to the circus last year James thinks anything that smells funny is clown food. Uncle Erwin, Mama's old old man, told James that one. Said clowns eat what the elephants leave behind.

They do, James said. That's why they look so funny.

Claude laughed, but he didn't laugh too hard. We could see it up ahead all black and dead, and we sure could smell it.

The grass was singed away to nubs by the flames, letting James' little body show again. The buildings sure didn't have no roof. There wasn't much left at all to speak of.

I told James to stay right with me. He held my hand tight. We walked right down the middle of what was them two buildings. There was hunks of burnt wood everywhere. Some picnic tables was lined up with the plastic tablecloths burned down on them for good.

Looky here, Claude said. He found him a cigarette machine and was kicking at it with his right boot. That door popped open and swung back and forth. There was cigarette packs scattered around the ground, but they was mostly burned up. Claude grabbed a pack of L&Ms out of the door and ripped them open. Anybody got a light? he asked, laughing at his own joke.

We must've pulled out twenty packs. There was Merits, Kools, Winstons. Some kinds we never heard of. Claude tore open a pack of Virginia Slims and stuck them all in his mouth at once. He dug my matches out of his pocket and lit the whole bunch up.

I looked around and James had got him some Marlboros. Put that down, James, I said. You got no business with that. He hugged the pack to his chest and said, I'm telling unless I keep it. He said he won't let Mama see nothing.

Claude unplugged the wad of cigarettes from his mouth and said, Let the boy have his smokes. Let the dying little man have his last wish. He probably won't even make it back home to tell your Mama anyway. Claude yanked one butt loose from the bunch, leaned over, and stuck it in James' mouth.

James didn't know whether to be scared or what. Anybody got a light? he whispered, smiling at Claude and letting that cigarette dangle from his mouth like Uncle Rooney used to do when he was trying to impress Mama. You best not be getting sick, I said. I swatted that butt from his mouth and pressed on it with my shoe until I was sure it weren't lit no more. I pushed James on past the picnic tables.

Those are where they took the women they bought, Claude said, lifting his eyebrows and pointing at a row of stalls with what was left of their doors going halfway up. I said it looks like where they kept the animals to me.

Clown food, James said, holding his nose.

Claude shook his head and pushed on a burnt door until it fell into two black pieces. A swarm of flies hit our faces. Claude batted them away and went inside. There was something curled up on the ground. A big lump of charcoal is what it looked like. It didn't have no hair left on it at all except down by its feet and the smell was something awful.

James started crying. He turned around and flew out of there. You get back here, I said, but he didn't listen. Claude poked the thing with his boot and it wiggled in a scary way. I wonder what it was, I said. Claude puffed up and said he bet his cousin knew her.

That's no woman, that's a goat or a dog or something, I said, gripping my arms tight to my chest.

Yeah, Claude grinned. I bet my cousin knew her, he said. We both smiled, but only for a second or two. Me and Claude got out of that stall pretty quick after that. He kicked that burnt thing again before he went out. He said it was like knocking on wood to keep the bad luck away.

I yelled for James, but there weren't no sound but the wind whipping through stirring up the ashes. Claude walked up ahead by some more picnic tables and his eyes lit up.

This here was where they did their drinking before they went off with the women, Claude said. Ralph told me about it. They'd bring bottles of whiskey in here with them or else they'd buy beer. Wait a minute.

Claude climbed over a counter and flipped up this metal lid. His head disappeared for a while, then he popped up with his hair all wet and water gray from ashes dripping down his face.

Are you crazy, Claude? I asked him. He smiled and lifted up a quart bottle of beer in each hand. We got us a party, he said, getting that crazy look again.

We heard some kind of shuffling noise and Claude pulled back on a door real quick. There was James all huddled up in a ball with his eyes shut tight. He started crying when we tried to grab him. Don't let it get me, Anthony. Keep it away from me, he said, curling up even tighter.

Don't say I didn't warn you, boy, Claude told him. But Claude helped me pull James out and dust him off.

We went and sat out in front on the burnt grass and James calmed down some. Claude lit cigarettes and passed one to me and one to James. James smiled and let the butt hang low in his mouth. Don't be inhaling none of that, I told him. He nodded his head up and down. It was real quiet.

Claude unscrewed the top on one of them beer bottles and took a swig. His coughed and handed it to me. It was warm and tasted like that medicine Mama gives me when I got the cold bug, only dangerous. I smelled that smell on Mama's old men before, the ones that started acting crazy, mostly.

James held out his hand for the bottle, but I shook my head and tightened my mouth. No, sir, I said. Not this time. James smiled and pushed that cigarette straight up toward his nose. I yanked some spider webs out of his hair and gave the bottle back to Claude.

We stared at some clouds floating by. Claude took another big swig on that bottle then sniffed at it some. He said he was trying to get the smell of that burnt thing out of his nose.

You figure it was alive before that fire hit? I asked. Claude rolled his eyes. What difference does that make? he said. It's sure dead now.

I wonder what it was feeling when the flames got to it, is all, I said. What it was thinking if it was still alive when things got hot.

It didn't think nothing, Claude said. It was a stupid old dog.

You'd think God could've put out that fire, I said. He could've saved that thing in there, whatever it was.

God don't got time to mess with everything, Claude said, handing the bottle back to me and leaning on his elbows. It's a big world out there and he got to let some things slide.

I asked Claude did he ever wonder why we was here. Claude said he wanted to see it. I said, no, no. Why we was really here.

God done it, James said.

Claude said there don't have to be no reason. You worry about that stuff and it'll drive you crazy in your head. You be like that thing in there, he said, pointing back at the building.

But don't he punish people who does wrong? I asked. Ain't life supposed to be special?

They go to hell. That's what the preacher say, James said, using his whole hand to hold that cigarette.

Claude shook his head. Life ain't too special around here, he said. My cousin Ralph said he saw a man get his ear bit right off back at that bar we was in. He said the waitresses squeezed the blood out of their aprons at the end of every night. No, sir, life ain't too special around here.

I handed the bottle back to Claude. He said it was ninety-nine percent spit, but he tipped the bottom up and drained it anyway.

The sun was almost straight over our heads. I said we best hurry James back before Mama gets home for dinner.

Claude tied them cigarettes up in the bottom of his shirt and asked if I was going to take any. I said I had me enough cigarettes for now. I grabbed the Marlboros from James and tossed them to Claude. James didn't complain none. His eyes was getting droopy.

Claude walked with us till we got out near the highway, then he went on through some tree branches and was gone.

Mama's car was in the driveway when we got to the house. I told James to wait outside till I was sure the coast was clear. I turned the knob real slow and eased the door in. Mama was sitting on the couch, but it was pulled out from the wall. She had my cigarettes and everything in a pile next to her, and her upper lip was curled down around her teeth. I looked back and James was right behind me staring in, all wide–eyed, too. I thought about telling him to keep his mouth shut, but then I knew that James had finally found him something he couldn't be a baby about and tell Mama. No, sir, he'd keep today locked inside of him for a long time. Maybe forever. ℘

THE SCREENWRITER

ON THE PATIENT SIDE of the hospice everything is white. A long, plain hallway with doors, some open, some closed; a curved nurse's station at the midpoint. As I approach it, I peek in an open door and spot an elderly woman sleeping, her mouth wide, her white hair an unruly sprig of cotton candy. The door to the baby's room is shut, and I'm glad of it. Death without a history is the cruelest joke of all.

Bob walks out of Mr. Wright's room carrying a bucket.

"Swabbing the deck," he says. "Hey, can you come around about four this afternoon? Dad should be awake and my sister will be there. She wants to meet you."

"It's a date," I say.

Room Eleven is open and I hear cartoon explosions on the television, so I walk in. The woman sleeping in the bed jerks up and down with each labored breath. An elderly man, whose dangling ears and droopy eyes remind me of the late President Lyndon Johnson, is sitting vigil with her.

"You're the writer." He takes off his glasses and examines me.

"Yes, sir."

"Pull up a seat and let's talk. I've got to tell somebody."

I scoot a chair over and notice the tears in his eyes. I squirm in my chair, on one hand fighting the urge to run from his grief and on the other guiltily ready to soak in the story.

"Fifty–eight years, five months, and five days." He wipes at the tears and replaces his glasses. "That's how long we've been married.

"Dorothy's my war bride. We met in New York City at a bar. She was only there because her friend Helen begged her to come."

"World War II?" I ask.

"The Big One," he says. "The bartender was a kid, so I got behind the bar and concocted the potions. Must have fooled her in my snazzy uniform because she stuck to me like glue. We sang all night. People used to really sing back then. Did you know that?"

"My father talked about it."

I don't add that he was often drunk at the time.

"Not like that rock stuff. The voices were pretty and soft."

"Sorry I missed that era."

Behind us her body heaves up and down. Her breathing is mechanical, desperate.

"She was a Yankee, but she loved me enough to come here to Texas after the war. It wasn't easy for her. We lived out in the country and she didn't have a lot of friends. Had our share of spats, but it was a good life. Four kids. All girls. They turned out all right."

"Any best memories?"

"I loved every minute with her." His eyes find mine. "She got me ready for this. Fixed my teeth. Moved us into a fancy retirement home with lots of widow ladies." The tears seep out from beneath his glasses. "This is the worst thing that's ever happened to me. I'm just glad she can't see what I'm going through."

He reaches over to the bed and gently strokes his wife's hand.

"Has she been sick long?" I can't think of any words that will ease his anguish.

"It was gradual. She fell a month ago and that was it. I couldn't take seeing her in the hospital. It killed me to see those tubes. Every time I turned around they were sticking her. We brought her here two days ago. My kids don't like it, say it's giving up."

I follow his eyes to the television where a commercial advertises a toy rocket that spins off into the sky.

"I can finally let my guard down," he says. "I didn't even feel it. Didn't realize how tired I was. My girls say I have a long life ahead. It won't be the same."

The door opens and a stumpy middle–aged woman walks in. She sits on the couch and stares at me.

"Emma, this is the writer," the old man says. "We're chatting."

"I'm not going to talk to you," she says. The words are matter of fact, but underneath them is the stab of an ice pick. The vulture has been exposed. I get up to leave.

"Thanks for listening, son," he says. "We'll muddle through."

I shut the door behind me and stand there for a moment, riding the crest of this wave of sadness. Near the nurse's station I rest on a couch. Across from me is a copy machine, to my left a door. Outside a woman sits at a picnic table smoking. I haven't had a cigarette in at least five years, but suddenly I feel the old desire gnawing.

A male nurse at the end of the hall starts walking toward me. I go the other way and seek out a patient I'd been warned about, one who is my age. The note on the door says his name is Fred Early.

The first thing I see in his room is the butterfly. The tattoo covers his back in a mix of green and blue and black. As I move quietly to the end of his bed, I see his body is curled around a brown plastic bucket.

"Hello," I say.

His head lifts from the sheet and he squints. His face is puffy and red, his eyes slits.

"You a cop?"

"No, a screenwriter."

"Yeah, they warned me about you. Don't mind the smell of my puke."

"I can handle it."

In truth the air has a sour sweetness that reminds me of a drunk waking up on a sewer grate. But I came here for death, and this is it.

"I can't. Haven't eaten in days, don't want to. But still this shit comes up smelling like skunk. Just my luck. You a lucky guy?"

"I'll never win the lottery."

"How's that?"

"Never bought a ticket."

"Lottery's a sucker's game," he says. "My wife CeCe said luck is a way of life. Having your eyes open. She figured unlucky people are too worried about the details to see the big picture, to see the big payoff staring them in the eyes. She's a scientist."

"How does your wife feel about this?" I ask.

Fred's body tenses at the question and convulses out a blast of bile. It sprays in the bucket and his head jerks back from the smell. It reeks of rotten fruit and urine.

His eyes are a red crisscross of anger and fear. "I don't want to talk to you. Get."

I quickly retreat, but, from the doorway, I risk one last look back at him. The butterfly is shuddering from a new convulsion. It's as if it's trying to rip itself free from his body.

His head turns slightly. His voice is soft.

"You want to know about my wife CeCe, then I got to tell you about my no–good father. It was at his house that all my problems started." ઌ

THE GAMBLER

WHEN WE PULLED UP to the trailer house, Crazy Baby was naked, robotically swinging a suitcase and pacing the roof. I wondered what the odds were of her falling off before she froze to death. Probably low; schizophrenics have a great sense of balance.

My wife CeCe glared at me and shook her head slowly. Her eyes, with their cool logic, said it all, but her mouth made it official. "This is your last chance, Fred, you wienerhead."

I reached for her hand and she squeezed mine back a little too tightly. Then Crazy Baby stood still and looked our way.

"George Washington can't get away with it," she screamed in a fast monotone, staring right through CeCe and me. "My stepfather kicks his dog and that dog don't bark at all. Them nurses try to touch me again and I'll sue them a new asshole. George Washington thinks he's got me fooled with that curly hair ..."

My mother used to say change is bad because it shakes things up too much. I suppose it's like spinning dice. Only the cheat knows which way the numbers fall. For me and CeCe, the dice were tumbling to the shrill sound of Crazy Baby. In charge of the game was the father who had left me with a legacy of self–doubts, and the group of mentally ill ex–convicts he tended in exchange for their monthly government checks. Trailers full of these outcasts of society circled Dad's house, like wagons holding off an Indian attack. I hadn't seen him in five years when he walked out the door.

"Baby, get your fat ass down here and take your meds," he said in a loud scratch, hands on his hips. Dad looked like how I imagined James Dean would if he'd made it to middle age: thick in the middle, wavy silver hair, dark glasses, an attitude.

"Got an itch to gamble, do you, boy?" he said without looking at me. Crazy Baby crawled down from the roof and Dad handed her a pill. Yeah, gambling reduced me to this. It started with a friendly poker game among high school classmates. It wasn't long before I was begging farmers for bets at a chicken fight. Last week they repossessed CeCe's Toyota from the front of the lab where she worked as a technician identifying viruses for fifteen bucks an hour. If they hadn't outright fired her after I showed up and she started punching and screaming, I'd wager she wouldn't be standing next to me now.

"Don't you mind Baby," Dad said and laid a hand on CeCe's shoulder. "She's just a dumb old crazy girl who likes to talk when she's off her pills. She's not used to a pretty woman like you."

CeCe smiled for the first time in days. CeCe was tiny, about four foot–eleven, but her piercing green eyes and erect posture made me forget I was a foot taller.

"I think she has maybe two synapses firing," CeCe said and pointed.

Crazy Baby searched her suitcase, pulled out a soiled dress.

"There's some kind of fire in Baby, that's sure," Dad said. "I'm Eugene Early, Fred's Papa. Looks like he won at something at least once. Come in and I'll show you around the mansion."

The two of them went giggling into the house and I was left standing there with Crazy Baby, who pulled a dozen stuffed animals out of the suitcase one at a time.

"These are my babies." She spit the words at me. "Don't touch them."

Dad once said she bit the ear off a fellow inmate who tried to take one of the dolls. Crazy Baby hadn't changed a lot since. There was a sprinkling of gray in her greasy hair and maybe a few more scars on her arms.

ᔕ ᔕ ᔕ

Dad did three things the year he decided to become Born Again: he adopted Crazy Baby, fresh from her parole; named his halfway house Tiresias Place; and invited me to visit. I didn't know what to make of his call. Mother had told me my father died in Vietnam. She'd remarried a good provider, a nice guy. My stepfather was always on the road, so I never knew him, and he sure wasn't the soldier Dad of my imagination. One spring break I'd even driven to the Vietnam Memorial and spent hours searching for Dad's name. My hero, my stability. Then I discovered he was an admitted murderer and con man who'd spent over twenty years behind bars. It was like I suddenly had a third arm, and it kept reaching up to slap me. I was fresh out of college then, one ball of contradictions.

"I don't apologize to nobody but God," Dad said during that first visit. He and Crazy Baby and I sat on his porch eating take–out chicken. Dad threw the bones to his pack of dogs, most of which seemed to be missing an eye, an ear, or a leg. "I ain't embarrassed to admit I fucked up, son. If you ever need me, I'm here on the bad side of town with people your Mama wouldn't let in the yard."

I nodded my head, chicken grease dripping down my lips, but inside I was running as fast as I could from Tiresias Place, my Dad, and his retarded, misshapen, adopted daughter.

ℭℭℭ

I had sworn I'd never be back, but here I was, penniless.

"Are you the doctor?" Crazy Baby asked in a child's voice. To her everyone was an authority figure. She couldn't keep them straight, but at least under medication she was coherent. "Cause you know I'm crazy. As can be."

She laughed and coughed at the same time, and smothered her mouth in a plastic doll's yellow hair. Crazy Baby peeked over the doll's head, her eyes full of mischief.

ℭℭℭ

"It all makes sense now, Fred," CeCe said in the dark.

After he'd introduced us to the rest of the residents, Dad had moved us into a trailer that smelled of Oreos and piss. It was crowded with mismatched furniture donated by churches. I squirmed next to CeCe's warmth, avoiding the random lumps on the mattress.

"What's that?" I asked.

"Why you are what you are."

"CeCe, please."

Once again I failed to read the signs. I saw sevens and elevens, but life was giving me snake eyes.

"You fooled me, Fred. When we got married I thought you had some kind of plan. I knew you had a hard time keeping a job, but I thought you were just creative. Then I realized you had Cheese Whiz for brains."

She reached over and ran her fingers through my hair. CeCe's strange speech patterns were endearing at first, but they did begin to grate.

"Let's not fight," I said and roughly patted my hair back into place.

CeCe didn't argue like a normal person. She was as predictable as a computer.

"Fred, when I met your father today the axiom became clear. He's just like you."

"He's not the least fucking bit like me, CeCe. That man killed somebody over a parking space. The guy cut in front of him and Dad pistol–whipped him until his nose collapsed. Tell me I'm like that, go ahead."

CeCe scooted closer and massaged my stomach.

"It's not so bad. Eugene's a charming man and kind of cute, too."

"Damn it, CeCe," I said half–heartedly.

"What I figured out," she whispered in my ear, wrapping a tiny leg around my waist, "is that you're a poor cultivar. That's all there is to it."

"CeCe, speak in English please."

She was lulling me to a comfortable excitement. Making love with her was like a long, hot bath.

"You're a poor cultivar. Like a variety of orange that didn't quite work. One that has hardly any flavor, brittle seeds, a thin skin. You see, I can't be too mad since it's in your genes."

I didn't know whether to be insulted or relieved. My wife just told me I'm inbred, but since she had the bad fortune to place her chips on me she would have to let it ride. Her logic was sexy.

ఌ ఌ ఌ

"I'm sorry about your mother," Dad said. He, CeCe, and I were sitting around a card table in his living room sipping coffee. Crazy Baby was on the floor shredding the day's newspaper. There was a dark mustiness to the house that made it clear this was home. The carpet was a thick maroon, and black velvet paintings of Jesus covered the walls.

"That she's dead or she's my mother?" I said.

CeCe flashed me a look. I meant the remark to come out jokingly. I buried mother two years ago, but she still was around passing judgment, telling me to quit making such a mess.

Dad just laughed and grinned. His eyes remained hidden behind dark glasses.

"Best stop sassing your Papa or I'll sic Baby on you. She's unpredictable." He swung around in his chair. "Tell him how crazy you are, honey."

Crazy Baby looked up from the mound of shredded paper.

"Who's he?"

"This here's an inspector from human services. Ugly, ain't he?"

"Nah, he's pretty," Crazy Baby said and fluttered her eyelashes.

Dad made up roles for me when one of the Tiresias Place residents came around asking for medication, cigarettes, or a few dollars for junk food at the 7–Eleven down the block. Most of the time they stayed in their trailers or sat out front. But when they did come to Dad's, I was a health inspector or a private investigator. Sometimes I was just another person over the brink.

"You ashamed to admit I'm your son?" I asked Dad just to goad him, to shuffle the deck.

"He's kidding, Fred. Quit the harangue."

CeCe stared at Crazy Baby with clinical fascination.

"That's all right, darling." Dad leaned into my face. He smelled of sweat and aftershave. "Boy, I admit you don't have a lot to recommend you. You got no money, no job, and a wife that's pissed. But we don't judge people. Me and God just kick ass."

Dad was puffed up, showing off for CeCe and making me feel like a kid. He called himself Born Again, but I was never sure if the religion was a scam. Being around Dad was like sticking your hand in a pit bull's mouth.

I watched as Crazy Baby jammed wads of newspaper into her mouth as if they were cotton candy.

"CeCe, honey, you know about Tiresias, the one I named this place for?"

Dad put his hand on her knee. He was trying to see if he could make me jealous, the crazy old fart. It was working; a heat was rising, but damned if I'd let him know.

"I assume that's a god. I'm not indoctrinated in mythology."

CeCe stared at a jagged scar across his knuckles. I realized—CeCe probably did, too—that this was the same hand that had gripped the gun when he'd killed that driver.

"No, he wasn't a god, but the gods blinded him. They felt bad about it, so they gave him the power of prophecy. That's like our Baby here. She don't have a lick of sense, but don't let it fool you. She knows more than she's letting on. Ain't that right, Baby? Tell this policewoman what you know."

Crazy Baby rocked back and forth and laughed. A drop of saliva, gray from the newsprint, hung from her bottom lip. "I didn't hurt nobody," she said. "They said they'd give me candy, but they didn't. I didn't hurt nobody."

Dad went to the kitchen and opened a drawer packed with oversized lollipops. He offered a green one to Crazy Baby. She moved to the corner and sucked.

CeCe rolled her eyes at me and motioned toward the door with her nose. I wanted to get out of this room—and Tiresias Place—but until one of us got a job we were stuck. I shrugged and Dad came back.

"You want you a lollipop, too, boy?"

He grinned at me and dropped a red sucker in the center of the table. I ignored him and watched Crazy Baby attack the dissolving green. There was no pattern; for a moment she licked the lollipop, then she nibbled at the edges, then she scraped her teeth along the sides.

"She did hurt them, but I don't know if she remembers," Dad said softly, as if confiding a deep secret, and leaned back until his chair tilted. "Me and Baby know what it means to put a world of hurt on somebody. She's simple–minded and them high school boys played with her. They was young and horny. One of them's a vegetable now. That's why I keep plenty of candy around. I ain't stupid, son."

He winked at me and I felt the hair on my forearms rise.

ග ග ග

"Maybe we should have a child," I said.

The thought popped into my head like a hunch on a horse. CeCe and I were watching *Leave it to Beaver* on a little black–and–white TV. I was spending a lot of time in our trailer, doing my best to avoid the old man. CeCe went out in the mornings to look for a job while I placed bets with myself on when she would return. When I peeked out the window, Crazy Baby was in the yard staring at me.

"Maybe you should get your rear end off the couch and go with me to look for a job," CeCe said. "I may find one and not come back."

"Take a chance on me, CeCe. Somehow I know if we have a kid, everything will work out."

I don't know where the idea came from, but at that moment I was sure. A kid would bond CeCe and me, force me to get responsible, force us to get away.

"Fred, you don't live on a plane of reality," CeCe said. "Remember I told you what my embryology professor said? If a tall person and a short person breed, their offspring can have disproportionate body parts. I will not bring some huge–headed child into this world to suffer. And you are not the best breeding stock."

Dad again. Everything returned to him. CeCe and I were like another pair of crazy people at Tiresias Place, dependent. He gave us money for gasoline and food, invited us to church, cooked dinner every Friday. I wondered when he would offer up lithium. Dad was steadily gaining control. I was sure that at some unexpected moment he would shake us like dice in his scarred hands and send our lives spinning. He was always touching CeCe.

"Do you think he and Crazy Baby do, you know, *it*?" I asked.

CeCe squeezed her mouth into an O shape. "You're sick, Fred. Get off Eugene's cloud. He did some horrible things, but with age there is mellowing. He does take care of misfits. That should count."

I sunk down into the couch. "It should, but you can't take everything at face value, CeCe."

CeCe smiled. "Now you're talking," she said.

∽ ∽ ∽

The menu was meat loaf smothered in blood red barbecue sauce. CeCe cut hers into neat squares and placed them in her mouth one by one. Dad shoveled the crumbling meat in. Crazy Baby was on the floor leaning slightly against my leg. Sauce dripped from her mouth onto her T–shirt, but she kept her free arm tightly wrapped around a one–armed doll.

"What do you think, boy? Can the old man cook or what?"

His glasses slipped down and I saw his watery eyes for a moment before his forefinger replaced them with darkness.

"It's the first gamble I've taken in a while, Dad."

He laughed and CeCe pinched my thigh approvingly under the table. For a moment we could have passed for a happy family.

"You miss it, don't you, son? You got that itch in you and it won't go away." He was playing the understanding father. "I used to have that wildness, too. It's so strong." Dad leaned back in his chair. "You can taste it in your mouth and it tingles down." He looked up at CeCe. "It's like really fine sex, if you'll pardon the comparison, darling. Hey, wait a minute. I got me an idea."

Dad got up and returned with an ancient board game in a box.

"Monopoly," he said. "You can lose money and it won't matter one bit."

CeCe snickered. "Let's live dangerously."

Dad set the board on the table. It was yellowed with age and the tokens were heavy cast iron. It must have been donated to him by some church patron who found it disintegrating in an attic. I chose a man on a bucking steer as my token. Dad was the top hat and Crazy Baby the thimble. CeCe pulled an earring shaped like a butterfly from the box and used it. I went first and the dice snapped in my hands like old friends. Double threes. Oriental Avenue in the low rent district. It was mine for $100. Roll again. A one and a trey. Jail, just visiting. The man behind bars stared out.

"Come to visit Papa, have you, boy?" Dad said. He didn't smile. "You look right at home there. Hand over them dice."

Dad rolled a five and bought Reading Railroad; then CeCe rolled a six and owed me $6 rent.

"Oh, take your money, jackass," she said and nudged me in the ribs.

CeCe helped Crazy Baby roll the dice and they came up snake eyes. Community Chest. Doctor's fee, pay $50. The story of her life.

"Put the money in the middle and whoever lands on Free Parking gets it," CeCe said, and Crazy Baby complied.

The dice were mine. Hot hot hot. A five and a four. New York Avenue. $200. Mine, all mine. Just a square away from Free Parking. I was on a roll. I could feel it building. Boardwalk would be my next buy. More than anything I wanted to win. Dad's face gave nothing away.

Two hours later CeCe went bankrupt and the pot in the middle of the board had grown to massive proportions. She helped Crazy Baby barely stay in the game. Dad and I were amassing armies of houses and hotels. Crazy Baby landed on my Boardwalk and it cost her $2,000. I chuckled as CeCe mortgaged the rest of Crazy Baby's properties.

"That's not nice, Fred," CeCe scolded. "It's just a game."

"She's right, boy," Dad said and tapped his scarred hands on the table. "It's a game, and you're a loser. You done lost at everything up to now, haven't you? No point in changing."

He was trying to psych me out. I wouldn't let it work. "You're crazy, old man. Once I win that pot in the middle, you'll be dead."

Round and round the board our tarnished metal tokens went, but no one stopped on Free Parking. I kept landing on Baltic Avenue and paying $450 a shot to stay in Dad's fleabag hotel. It was too close to real life. I was almost broke.

Dad grinned at me and crossed his arms at his chest.

"Every since you been here you've been pushing, boy. Thinking you're better than your ex–con Papa. Well, it's time you learned a lesson." His grin was fluorescent. "I tell you what. You hit that pot in the middle, I'll give you real cash for the fake stuff and you can get your ass out of here. Maybe do some real gambling."

CeCe put her hand up, palm toward me as if she were trying to stop an oncoming train.

"Sounds like a plan, Dad."

CeCe's mouth was open, but she didn't say anything. She reached down and stroked Crazy Baby's head.

"But what happens if I lose?" I asked.

Dad wagged his tongue against his upper lip, his imagination hurtling through space.

"Boy, you lose and me and CeCe go into my bedroom for a few hours and see what comes up."

All expression was hidden behind his dark glasses. CeCe flinched. I looked in her eyes and swore I saw fear and a little anticipation.

She said, "That's not funny, Eugene," and started laughing. But she stopped when I said, "Okay." It came out before I could stifle it—instinct. The pot on the table must have topped $5,000. I had been hot all night. I needed a seven to take it all. I couldn't lose.

CeCe stared at me wide–eyed, as if I were an experiment gone horribly awry.

I started rattling the dice in my cupped hand.

"Fred," CeCe said flatly, her green eyes flaring. "I'll hate you till hell freezes over and that ought to be about the time you get there."

I couldn't hear her anymore. The bones were spinning like fire in my palm. Round and round they went. Faster and faster. Finally, they left my hand like slow–motion rockets and skidded across the board. At the far side one careened against Dad's top hat and skipped off the table toward the carpet. Crazy Baby rose like a whale from the depths and sucked the flying dice into her lips. She puckered up and sent it sailing back to the board. The saliva–covered dice had five dots showing, the one that didn't get away had two. A winner, but it didn't count.

"You can't even keep it on the table, boy," Dad said and leaned in toward me as he got up out of his chair. "Let me get a towel to clean up your mess. Excuse me, CeCe, darling."

CeCe nodded mechanically, but her eyes were fixed on me the entire time.

"It's no big deal," I told her. I could feel the sweat drip down my forehead and collect in my eyebrows. "I'm going to win. I'm due. Then we can escape from this place. It's a sure thing."

CeCe rubbed her fingers lightly across Crazy Baby's head.

"Your expiration date is showing, Fred," CeCe said flatly.

Dad walked back in holding a kitchen towel with brownish stains on its edges and the faded words "God Bless This Mess" across it.

"Here, boy," he said and tossed the towel at me.

Dad stood behind CeCe's chair and rested his meaty hands on her shoulders. He methodically massaged them, only the thin layer of blouse separating him from her. CeCe smiled toward me, though her lips remained tightly clenched together.

"God does love a sinner," Dad said. "Now roll them dice and let's see what he has in store."

I rubbed Crazy Baby's saliva off the dice and picked up its companion. The bones felt sticky in my palm. I used wrist action to spin them around—that's the secret for a good toss. I kept flicking my wrist up and down and the dice click click clicked. They became an extension of me, cubes of flesh. If I squeezed one at that moment, I was sure it would bleed and I would feel the pain.

"He does have style."

Dad ran his hand along CeCe's neck. She didn't flinch, just stared intently at my hand as if it were under a microscope.

My wrist was getting sore from the movements, but the dice weren't ready to stop. My hand jerked up and down, up and down. Everything else receded from view. My palm was hot from the friction of the spinning dice. My breath came out loud and labored. My fingers finally pried open, and the dice spilled across the board. I went limp and closed my eyes tightly. When I opened them, I saw a three and a four. I had won. The gamble had finally paid off. I instinctively reached out my sore hand and caressed the pile of fake cash that would soon be real.

"Jesus loves you, son," Dad said, and let his hands fall from CeCe's shoulders. "You count it all up and I'll write you a check. Y'all can cash it in the morning."

"Better split it into two checks, Eugene," CeCe said and took Dad's right hand in hers. Her face was wet with tears. "I believe this is a community property state."

"Sure, honey," Dad said. "Why you come up to my room and I'll write it for you now. We'll estimate."

CeCe stumbled as she got out of her chair, but reached out a hand and steadied herself on Crazy Baby's shoulder.

"CeCe," I said, staring in disbelief. "What are you doing? I won. Do you understand? I won. This doesn't make sense. With him?"

She reached across the table and slapped me.

"I've told you before, Fred—for every action there is a reaction. This one's mine. I'm taking the car in the morning. What I do until then is none of your concern. And who says I'm doing anything? Face facts, Fred. At least Eugene does that."

The two of them walked up the stairs, CeCe leading, as I sat there trying to think of something to say—anything.

"Fair is fair, Dad," I finally said in a pleading whine. "I won."

He looked back over his shoulder from the top of the stairs, tilted his glasses down so I could see his smiling eyes, and said, "That's right, son. You did. When you get that money counted, yell that figure up to me. Or come visit us if you dare to take another risk."

They reached the top of the stairs and disappeared from sight. I heard a door open and loudly shut. I sat there numbly with my winnings, then Crazy Baby nudged my leg. She held her doll tightly to her chest and reached down to kiss its forehead. Crazy Baby looked up at me and smiled angelically, her eyes daring me to reach out and wrench the plastic baby from her arms. ☙

THE SCREENWRITER

I GO HOME FOR lunch, and my sister Sara is waiting outside. I've told her vaguely what I'm up to, hanging out with dying people. Sara's a paramedic so she filled me in on her other experiences seeing people die. We both were there when our Dad passed.

She examines me like I'm a broken piece of pottery, like she's waiting for the water to start seeping through my cracks. Sara places something in my palm. A small metal shape.

"A pocket angel," she says. "To protect you."

I rub it between my fingers. Sara and I haven't talked much lately, and I feel guilty again for abandoning her so often since Dad died.

"I'm going to regift this," I say. "A man at the hospice."

"Is he dying?" she asks.

"Yeah. He needs it more than I do."

∽∽∽

I get back to the hospice a lot earlier than I'd planned, figuring I'll take some time to observe the place before going to see Mr. Wright. Sit back and take it in without talking to anybody for once. My screenplay needs what the pros call synergy, a system, some way to pull all of the pieces together like a skeleton. How can it have shape when I'm not even sure where this is headed? I've got to figure that out.

In the waiting room I see the woman from earlier, the one who wouldn't talk to me, the one who identified me as the interloper. She's sardined onto a couch with a round–faced man and a fidgety group of children picking at their dress clothing. Her ear is glued to a cell phone and she is nodding

She spots me, puts her hand over the phone and says, "My mother died."

The words wash over me and I wonder again if this is worth it.

"Is your father OK?" I ask.

"He's in there with her now," she says. "Listen, the reason I wouldn't talk to you before. There's more to it that you don't know. Family stuff."

"I'm sorry for your loss."

The words sound artificial, memorized. A eulogy for a woman I didn't know. A body disintegrating on the bed while I watched and listened. Can I even remember her name? Dorothy. Her name was Dorothy.

I bolt toward the patient wing. Anywhere to avoid this family's grief. But it travels down the hall with me, wraps around my legs, and clings.

I sink into the couch, wait for 4 p.m. to meet Mr. Wright's daughter and watch. Three nurses are at work today. Two tinker behind the desk while the third disappears into rooms. Then they all get up and leave. Moans from down the hall. A cafeteria worker in a plastic hairnet pushes a cart of food trays. Soft footsteps on tile. A boy lugs three cases of soft drinks in, drops them behind the counter, and leaves. A bony woman, her fingers clotted with jewelry, places flowers in vases around the room. Red, pink, purple.

Smell is supposed to be the strongest of our senses, evoking memories and emotions. I sniff the air. What does this place smell like? Not a hospital, but not death either. It's like a birthday cake studded with candles that no one ever got around to lighting.

A creak and a thud. I look to my right. The door eases open and then slinks back. Back and forth, back and forth. I lean over and peer out at the smokers' picnic table. No one is there. I consider shutting it, but don't. I'm an observer today. Obeying the code of noninterference like on old *Star Trek* episodes. BAM! The door slams closed and stays that way. The sound reverberates.

I look up on the wall above the photocopier and spot a small sign I hadn't noticed before. It's a diagram of all of the emergency exits. At the top it says EVACUATION PLAN. I have my screenplay title, and I know who just left the building. Goodbye, Dorothy. Happy trails.

Two men come to the counter and wait for a nurse. One is old, white, and droopy; the other is young, brown, and tall. They both wear dark blue suits and are clutching green plastic wristbands. The looks on their faces are grim but not unhappy. "I'm sorry for your loss." That's what it says. The artificial words of an undertaker or a stranger like me. "I'm sorry for your loss, but please sign here. And here." Then the body will be whisked efficiently out the back door and into a shiny hearse. Embalming ho!

The young Latino clasps his hands in front of him, and his head tilts forward. It's almost as if he's praying. ↀ

THE MORTICIAN

MAGGIE'S EYES WERE LIKE the creek water, muddy green and shiny with mystery. I watched her lift her boob and squeeze it.

"They dribble," she said. "It's not milk, Henry. More like water."

She crossed her arms underneath and lifted them high. She squinted at me again. I couldn't tell if she was happy, pissed off, or if the sun was in her eyes. Maggie was changing fast. We both were. Soon our baby would arrive.

It was Maggie's idea to hang out at Esperanza Hole, like old times. She was busy with high school and being pregnant and I had my job at the restaurant on Sixth Street. No time to be kids no more, she said. Our crowd had come here all the time last summer to escape the heat. Now it rained and our friends were busy partying.

Maggie waded into the murky water until her tummy disappeared. She looked brand new.

∽ ∽ ∽

I had hooked up with her in Freddy's laundry room, out back of his parents' house. Me and Freddy were there with his girlfriend Cassandra and Maggie and this little runt Tomas. Freddy's parents were squawking at him about something or other—taking the trash out or studying. I don't remember. So Freddy dragged us out to the garage where they got their laundry room and said why don't we play Truth or Dare.

Tomas was a zit–faced retard and he asked what that was. Freddy said it's a game, and we sat down to play. Maggie slid down across from me and she was wearing one of those half shirts that exposed her belly piercing—she took it out when she found out about the baby. She wouldn't look right at me, but when she smiled the corners of her eyes crinkled in a sexy way I'd never noticed at school.

Freddy turned out the light and left us in shadows from the porch light outside. He pointed at Tomas. "Truth or dare?"

"Truth," Tomas said.

"You ever kiss a girl?"

Tomas' lips got tight. "Yeah."

"Not related to you?" Freddy asked.

Tomas slumped his shoulders forward. "No." The word came out like he was confessing to a priest.

Freddy's girlfriend Cassandra leaned over and gave Tomas a wet one, tongue and all. "He has now," she said, and laughed at Freddy.

Cassandra had big lips and a giant mound of woolly hair. She shook her head toward Freddy in challenge and her hair hardly moved.

I watched the color inch up Freddy's neck as he gave her the evil eye. Freddy turned to Tomas and said it was his turn, all business–like.

Tomas pointed at Maggie and squeaked, "Truth or dare?"

"Dare," she said and folded her arms at her chest. She wasn't falling for that truth stuff.

"Stick your hand down Henry's pants and leave it there for three minutes." He turned to Freddy for approval, and Freddy slapped him on the back and yelped like they were best buds.

Maggie scooted across the concrete floor to me and eased her soft fingers under my blue jeans. Nobody else moved. She looked into my eyes and I saw she was not afraid. Maggie grabbed onto the curly hair up high and gripped it. She put her head on my shoulder and we all sat there silent in the semi–dark waiting. I never wanted those three minutes to end.

ꟹ ꟹ ꟹ

The back road to Maggie's house was winding and surrounded by cows. A skunk was smooshed next to the center stripe and the stink filled my car.

"Hold your breath," Maggie said.

"Too late."

"No, not that. The Holy House. Hold your breath."

I slowed the car to thirty and turned into the curve. Next to the main part of the bend was a wooden home that had been slammed into so many times that the owners had given up trying to fix it. There were about three layers of corrugated metal tacked on the gash, but they hung there like rusty Band–Aids. The fence around the yard swayed in the breeze like it was cobwebs. Inside it was a rusty swing set.

"Let us pray about bad feng shui," Maggie said.

"Amen," I said and held my breath.

As we passed I saw a guy on the porch watching us, his cowboy boots propped on the rail. We completed the turn and the house disappeared. Maggie and I opened our lungs and took in fresh skunk air.

We went through this routine every time I took her home. She saw something about the feng shui stuff on TV. It basically meant they screwed up big time to put a house in the middle of that nasty curve. They were asking for it.

Maggie's dad was standing out by his Winnebago when we pulled up. He nodded at me and it was like it hurt his neck to move that much. He had told Maggie that I ruined his retirement. He and Maggie's mama were planning to load up the big bus and travel. Except Maggie's mama never wanted to go. Now they were meeting with my mother, stockpiling baby clothes and diapers, making plans.

"Shouldn't be running around with the little one coming," her old man yelled.

Maggie stuck her tongue out at him.

"I'm about to pop, Henry," she said and kissed my cheek. "When we getting an apartment?"

"Soon," I said.

The old man helped her out of the car. He turned to me and winked.

"Sooner than you think, vato," he said and slammed the door. "Puppy love don't got nothing to do with babies."

"Leave him alone, Papa." Her hand slid down my arm and gave me goose bumps.

I watched Maggie waddling up the walk with the old fart. He was one of them big–gut construction workers and tried for a while to talk me into joining his crew. No way. As I put it in gear and headed toward Austin, I tried to remember the feel of Maggie's fingers tugging on my pubes. I tried to memorize it.

∽ ∽ ∽

"Run!" Vernon screamed as I cut through the kitchen and down the alley to the parking lot with car keys rattling in my palm. I heard his laughter echoing in the clink of metal pots and pans behind me. It was a red BMW. The hard part was figuring out the little differences. Some had a button you got to push to get the keys out. Took me thirty minutes in one fancy car and the dude was P.O.'d. No tip.

My manager Vernon was an old guy in his forties and said my job was good training for life. Most of the time I stood around out front watching the Sixth Street party crowd, daydreaming, keeping the stinky old street drunks shooed away. Then, bang, a customer needed action and I ran like a gazelle across Africa.

I pulled the BMW up to the curb and a big college boy palmed me a single like it was a candy bar. His lady was too skinny and too blonde, but she rubbed her arm against mine as she slid past and a sweet coconut smell climbed into my nose. Her boyfriend slammed the door and gunned the engine.

"Watch out for Hawk," Tony said from the oyster bar just inside the front door. "Gonna get in a tussle with Mr. Muscle."

"Nah." I shook my head from the open doorway. The guys at the restaurant all called me Hawk because of my nose. You couldn't miss it.

"Ladies love our Hawkie," Tony said and used the metal cracker to slam apart another oyster shell. Tony meant everything he said, so I know he wasn't just razzing me. Tony was a truth–teller. He even spent six months in a monastery. A pale black guy with a thinning Afro who was addicted to video games and called himself a professional college student. That was all there was to Tony. Nothing to hide.

"No lie, Hawk," Tony said. "Ask Webster. The bubba's back from Los Angeles, so he knows the score."

Webster unloaded a tray of shark steaks on table seven and walked our way.

"You want to know the truth about Cali?" Webster was a surf punk from Corpus Christi majoring in business at U.T. Always told me to take the G.E.D. and move on up. Me dropping out of high school was no biggie to him. Just another step in life's forward plan.

"Tell Hawk the ladies love him," Tony said and handed Webster a tray of a dozen oysters on the half shell.

"It's that long old Indian nose," Webster said. "Dude gives them ideas. And they can sniff the vibe that he's under contract to Daddytown."

"Tell me about California," I said. My mind begged to travel like Webster, to go to a monastery with Tony. Just be anywhere but the same old, same old.

"Cali," Webster said and adjusted his red apron. "Here's something Swami Tony will groove on: in California you can only turn right and there's only one way out of every parking lot. Think about it." He turned and glided the oyster tray across the room like he was riding the perfect wave.

Tony grinned and pointed outside.

A red Corvette idled at the curb. I ran–walked to it and eased the driver's door open. A round Arab man slid loose. He was alone and his car smelled of leather cleaner and Old Spice.

"My friend, twenty dollar tip if you get me a parking spot on Sixth Street for the night." His eyes were droopy and he gave my white shirt and bow tie the once over. "I plan to party hearty in the clubs tonight. Understand?"

"Sure," I said and he shoved a five–dollar bill in my shirt pocket. "This is for starters, my friend. Scoot."

I got behind the wheel and took the loop. Down to Congress, around to Fifth and back up Sixth. The seat was low to the ground and cradled my back. I took it slow and pretended I was a rich A–rab. A tall redhead in a top hat and short–shorts blew me a kiss from her stool outside a bar, and I whistled back at her. In the rearview I saw an older couple walking up to their car. I slammed on the brakes, turned on the emergency flashers and hopped out after them. The car behind me honked, but I ignored it and kept moving.

"Pay you five bucks if you hold that spot till I get around the block," I said.

The stringy old guy put his hand on his hip, thought about it for too long and said, "Sold."

ಌ ಌ ಌ

"You're yellow," my boss Vernon said.

I shrugged and swiveled my head trying to look around my shoulder.

"Wear a new shirt tomorrow." He shook his head and straightened a stack of menus by the hostess table. The girl who was supposed to be in tonight quit, and Vernon was grumbling about having to seat people.

I went through about three shirts a month. The sweat stains didn't come out and it was eating up my paycheck something awful.

"Two?" Vernon said. I looked up and it was Tomas with some squat girl from school. She and I had had algebra together before I hooked it out of there.

Tomas gave me that sly look like saying, "Are you going to give me a discount or what?" I knew he couldn't afford our prices.

"I'll take this one." I grabbed two menus and led them to surfer dude's section where I knew he'd treat them right.

Tomas was looking good, actually. His acne was down to a low hum and he was in a blue suit jacket and khaki pants, like the salesmen wear at the mall. His shirt was crispy white.

"We're celebrating," the girl sing–songed when I got them seated under a plastic marlin.

Tomas nodded. "I got accepted."

I didn't know what he was talking about, but I was used to that, so I just nodded.

"College," the runty girl said. "It's in California."

"Where you can only turn right and there's only one way out of every parking lot," I said, repeating Webster's words with no idea what they meant.

Tomas and the girl laughed.

"Is Maggie alright?" Tomas said. His hair was gelled up and spiked like out of GQ. He still looked twelve. But he was going to California.

"Yeah," I said. "Any day now."

"Baby," Tomas said to the girl in explanation and she got a big, goofy grin.

I slipped away while she was thinking what to say next and went on out the door. I leaned on the doorframe and waited for cars. The sun was going down and Sixth Street was waking up. A homeless drunk walked by cradling a retriever puppy and asked if I wanted to pet it. I stuck out my hand and the fur was soft like feathers.

"His name is Hound."

The guy's eyeballs were a mishmash of yellow and red and he smelled like piss, but I knew he meant no harm. I saw him out here a couple times a week, collecting cans to sell at the recycling center, bumming a dollar for a tallboy down at the liquor store. One time he showed up covered with bruises. Another drunk had beaten him up and stolen his cans.

The dog peered up at me and yawned. The drunk winked, tucked the dog under his dirty shirt, and waddled on down the road.

The cover band across the street was warming up. Stray notes floated my way as the streetlights came on and my shoulders slumped into the brick. It was an old song by Van Morrison. I hummed along, but I couldn't remember the name.

The artist was set up a few feet away and I could tell he was drawing me again. To get customers he had to already be at it, so his colored pencils were scribbling, probably concentrating on making my nose and bow tie huge. Everything's got to be funny but cute to satisfy the tourists, he'd told me once.

A family was hovering over the artist, pointing at me and laughing. It made me remember taking a train with Maggie's family to go ride the rides at Six Flags. I couldn't believe she was related to them. The main thing I remember was they smelled bad, not dirty bad but like moldy fear. Her uncles were bony with reddish tans and buzz–cut hair. Her aunts were round, with blonde hair and black roots, and cackled like crows at one uncle's jokes. "What do you call a cow with no legs? Ground beef. What's green and sings? Elvis Parsley."

Grandma paced the train aisle fingering a rosary while grandpa, a quiet man with a stringy comb–over, kept the grandkids busy. When she looked at him it was with pure hate. He stared into his hands. Then the grandkids started crying all at once like baby birds. Maggie gripped my hand tightly and the train kept aiming us toward Ferris wheels and roller coasters. I had gone home after that and kissed my mother. I'd have kissed my dad, too, but he died of cancer when I was twelve.

ᔓᔕ ᔓᔕ ᔓᔕ

"It's for you, Hawk." My manager Vernon was at the doorway with that look that said personal calls at work were a no–no.

Tony handed the phone across the bar and I sat in one of the tall chairs to take it. The restaurant was designed to look like a fancy boat. I stared at myself in the glass behind Tony and said, "Hello?"

"It's time, baby. Or I should say it's baby time."

The call was cloudy with static and I knew Maggie had to be on her old man's cell phone.

"You sure?"

Maggie sighed and laughed. "It's either that or I got one hell of a stomach ache."

I sat there for a couple of seconds too long not saying anything.

"Henry?"

"I'm here. I was thinking maybe we could move to California." It just popped out.

"California? We're having a baby. Now. Here. Texas." Her laugh was nervous, then muffled as she turned to her dad to say something. "Papa said no free baby–sitting in California."

Tony started popping oysters apart in front of me and the salty sea odor filled my nose. I wondered what the baby would smell like.

"What's green and sings?" I said and imagined myself on a train with one of Maggie's aunts.

"Henry, we're on our way to the hospital. You know the one?"

"By the interstate."

"Yeah. Meet us there."

"I gotta see if I can get off work."

Now Maggie got quiet. I could hear the moan of a train whistle through the phone.

"Elvis Parsley," I said.

"What?"

"That's what's green and sings."

"Go to the hospital." Her voice was flat and matter–of–fact. "The one by the interstate. I already called your mother and she's on her way."

"OK," I said.

"He's kicking. I can feel him begging to get out."

I fought back the urge to say I knew how he felt.

"I love you, Maggie," I said instead.

"I know, Daddy Henry. Hey, best excuse ever for not doing my homework, right? We're almost at the Holy House. Have to hold my breath. Gotta go."

She hung up in my ear and I could somehow see her Dad's van turning into the curve. I could see that guy in the cowboy boots on the front porch. I could feel our baby kicking.

"Bad news? Tony said.

I smiled a real smile. "I'm gonna be a daddy."

"Congrats again."

"No, right now."

"Hey, Webster," he shouted. "Hawk's baby is in the house."

"Don't seat it in my section. I got enough underage drinkers."

"I'm gonna be a daddy," I repeated for Webster. I realized I was smiling. Big. So big it almost hurt.

Vernon the boss grabbed my shoulder and said to get moving.

"He can still make a run for it," Webster said.

I flashed that the idea of a baby maybe scared him more than it did me.

"Cali. Mexico. Head for the hills before it's too late," Webster said. He was smiling now, razzing me. "Steal one of our customer's cars. You've got the keys, dude."

Tony plopped a tray of oysters on the table in front of me. I squeezed a lemon wedge on one and slurped it from the half shell.

"Oh, well, it's all good until Feb. 1, 2019," Webster said. "That's when the meteor hits."

"Crazy," I said.

"No, really, that's the prediction. As powerful as a nuclear bomb and nobody knows where it'll crash."

Tony nodded. "I heard about that. But they think it'll probably miss us completely. No reason to expect the worst."

"Live for today, baby," Webster said.

Vernon gave me a shove. "Clowns. Don't listen to them," he said. "Get going. I'll cover for you—this once."

Tony laughed. "Now that is a first."

I slid another oyster down my throat then took off running through the restaurant. Tony, Vernon, and Webster were quickly a blur. I glided past college–boy Tomas and his date, and on into the kitchen. The workers cheered for me, banging spoons against pots until the back door shut behind me. Around the dumpster, down the stinky alley, and onto the street. Bobbing and weaving around two drunk girls. I could feel the shirt sticking to my back. Past the lot where I parked other people's cars. My Impala was two blocks away and getting closer. My feet kicked up close to my butt as I put it into highest gear.

The lock on the driver's side didn't work, so I opened the other door and slid across. The drive to the hospital was easy, but it took forever. All the while I was driving, I was thinking: hop, shuffle, step. Slap. Ball–change. Tap dancing. Maggie was taking classes last year and showed me how. I could see her making the slow movements, only I thought she said ball–chain. I was going to be a father. It seemed crazy to even imagine. We wouldn't be like Maggie's grandma and grandpa. I knew that. Our boy (girl?) would smell like sweet corn tortillas and never worry a day in her (his?) life. Maybe in a couple of years we'd go to California together. Maggie and I'd teach her (him?) to tap.

The hospital door opened automatically. The lady at the front desk put down the telephone and looked at me like I was a science experiment.

"Having a baby?" she asked.

"Not me personally," I said and she laughed.

"It's written all over your face. Maternity is the fifth floor. Congratulations."

I got off the elevator and went down the hall where I found all the babies. They were behind glass, each one in a special little rocket ship–like crib with numbers and names scribbled on a little piece of paper stuck on the back. I leaned in close to see their wrinkly pink and brown faces. They were all crying mouths and dizzy eyes. I spotted an empty rocket ship and knew that one was for my kid. Blast off.

A nurse asked if she could help and I told her I was looking for Maggie. She and her dad weren't there yet, so she showed me where I could go get a Coke. I waited in a little room that had a couple of couches and a TV that was set on MTV. Girls in bikinis surrounding a swimming pool. A rap band on stage in front of them. Everybody smiling and being cool.

Aliens.

Hop, shuffle, step. Slap. Ball–change. Maggie's smile when she danced was what the bikini girls looked like. Everything concentrated on one thing. Being in the right place, doing everything perfect.

After awhile I got that feeling like I had to pee, and I realized I'd been waiting for a long time. On the TV, the dancers had been replaced with a car full of rappers flashing money and driving fast.

I got up to go find a nurse and my mom walked in. Her eyes were big and scared. She didn't have to tell me a thing.

"Maggie?" I asked.

"An accident. She and her daddy are…" Mom put her arm around me and squeezed. She was shaking. "There's no God, son. He wouldn't do this to us again."

"Holy House?" I said. "Did they hit the Holy House?"

Mom's lips sputtered. She must have thought I was nuts. "It was a drunk driver. He crossed over and hit them head–on."

I slapped my fist against my thigh.

"Baby?"

"Gone," she said. "I'm so sorry, Henry."

I looked in her eyes, and I could tell she was thinking of my dad. I was afraid to look too long, afraid she'd see the relief that I felt forcing its way up to mix with my tears.

She wiped my eyes with a tissue, and I shook my head.

"I got to go there," I said.

"They're gone, Henry," she said. "On their way here. It's all a mess. You're a baby yourself. It's not right."

"I got to go," I repeated, and turned and ran.

I took the stairs. My own car keys were jangling in my hand as I hopped down two, three steps at a time. It was like if I went fast enough I could outrun it. In school I learned that the streaks of lightning in the sky are plasma. That's what the sun and stars are made of, too. That's what I was thinking as I got in the car and started driving. I couldn't go fast enough.

Maggie had this way of moving her jaw when she was mad at me. It sort of popped in and out on the side as she gritted her teeth. I could see her doing that and holding her breath at the same time as her old man steered into the turn by the Holy House. I could see the small bulge of stomach bursting out above her bathing suit. Maggie was the one who told me women float easier in water than guys. "Boys are denser," she had said and fluttered her eyelashes. At least I told her I loved her. That had to count for something.

The lights on Highway 290 kept turning yellow as I got to them. Warning. Danger. I punched the pedal down as far as it would go and veered around slow–moving trucks. Fuckfuckfuckfuckfuckfuckfuck. This was not real. I kept expecting to see the ambulance on the other side of the road coming toward me with their bodies. I needed proof. I had to see it for myself. I considered veering into oncoming traffic and fought my hand not to turn the wheel. I wanted to turn the wheel.

I took a left onto the back road that led to Maggie's house and got ready for it. I remembered a rule by Newton, the apple guy, that I'd learned in driver's ed. He said if something was moving fast, it wouldn't stop until you put something in its way. I wanted to kill the guy who got in the way. If he was not already dead.

My headlights swept over something shiny and red by the side of the road. Broken glass? Was that what was left? It was her Dad's fault. He wasn't paying attention. No, it was my fault. I should have been driving her myself. It was Maggie's fault for leaving me behind. She was probably distracting her old man with baby talk. It was the baby's fault. The baby I'll never see.

In my mind I heard the words Mr. Dotson had kept hammering at us in driver's ed.: "Expect the worst possible outcome." I steered into the first curve and knew the Holy House was in the middle of the second one. They had gotten at least this far.

I thought maybe I should hold my breath for Maggie, but there was nothing there. I realized I hadn't been breathing at all. My chest was tight steel. I saw the front porch of the Holy House and stomped on the brake. My Impala pulled off onto the grassy shoulder of the curve, and I took the deepest breath I could. My lungs rejected it so I tried again and it worked. I looked over at the Holy House. I couldn't believe what I saw.

The cowboy was in the yard under a bright light, and I started giggling. Tears ran down into my eyes, but I couldn't stop. It was too ridiculous. I imagined Maggie perched in the seat next to me, laughing even harder, but I didn't dare look to see if she was there. Where the gash had been in the side of the house, the cowboy was now leaning over. He was holding a window frame and trying to set it just right. He was putting a window in at night! It made no sense, but I wanted Maggie to see it with me. This one last, weird moment. I felt her fingers stroke the back of my hand and imagined I heard a baby's gurgle. I reached out and gripped tightly, but she was gone. ☙

THE SCREENWRITER

BOB AND HIS SISTER wake me from a daydream, and I look out through foggy eyes. She's taller than her brother, younger looking and holds herself with the grace of a movie star.

"I'm Carla," she says. "I hear my father's smitten with you."

"Gross," Bob says.

"I mean in a socially acceptable, nonsexual, guys–watching–football kind of way," Carla says.

"I think he's pretty cool, too," I say.

She cocks her head at me in a friendly challenge.

'In a non–sexual, old–fart kind of way," I say.

"Ah. Just checking. I heard you're a writer, so we can't be too careful."

"Aren't you a writer, too?" I ask.

"Exactly," she says.

"She's a newspaper reporter," Bob says. "Do they really count?"

"Only to ten," she says.

ശ ശ ശ

Mr. Wright is sitting up examining a framed picture of Jesus on the wall when we come in.

"Matt! Where they hell you been, boy? A man could kick the bucket waiting for you to come calling."

"Many have," Bob says.

His sister kicks at Bob's shin but misses.

"True, true, true," Mr. Wright says. "I sense the ghostly apparitions wandering the halls bellowing, 'You call this a lunch?'"

"Sorry to be so tardy," I say. "Work called."

"Work," he says. "Life's big annoyance. But the right job can keep us sane, too. I learned that from the other Wright. Do you know his tragedy?"

"No," I say.

"Not that again, Daddy," Carla says.

"It's tearjerker time," Bob says.

"Bear with me, oh children of my loins," Mr. Wright says. "It seems Frank Lloyd left his wife and six kids for a woman named Mamah.

Built her the showpiece that is Taliesin. One night when he was abroad on a project, a butler Mamah had sacked earlier that day set the house on fire during Mamah's dinner party. The butler waited outside with an ax and chopped everyone to bits as they tried to escape."

"That's what happens when you abandon your kids." Carla winks at her father. "Karma."

"Ouch!" Mr. Wright stretches back onto the bed. "Guess I had that coming, dear one. Matt, you know what Frank Lloyd did after burying Mamah on the grounds?"

"Bet he didn't go back to his kids," Carla says.

"He rebuilt Taliesin! Better than it was before. You know why?"

"Ego?" Bob says.

"Indeed," Mr. Wright says. "He did it because that was his job. He was a goddamned architect!"

I can't help but look at Wright and his two wisecracking children and think of Sarah and me and the wall that separated us from our father. It's the same wall Charlie Wright claims stands between him and Bob, but I don't see it. This is a happy family.

"When do I meet your other son?" I ask.

Silence. They look at each other and seem to hold their breaths. Carla finally lets out a titter of a laugh.

"You've revealed the five–hundred–pound elephant lounging in the room," she says.

"Is that what I smell?" Bob says.

Mr. Wright closes his eyes. I notice his face is getting progressively paler with each of my visits. Suddenly he jolts upright.

"Open the goddamned sin … bin … window!" he yells.

I pull back the curtain.

"More like it," he says. "Frank Lloyd taught us that only savages hole up in the dark like inmates. In a free world, windows are where it's at. Light! Let there be light the way God planned it!"

I reach in my pocket and pull out the angel.

"This is for you," I say.

Mr. Wright holds it up and examines it.

"An angel?" he says.

"Yeah. It's called a pocket angel. Supposed to protect you."

He cradles it in his palm and his eyes fill with tears.

ꕥ ꕥ ꕥ

"He killed himself," Carla says.

Mr. Wright is sleeping and Bob has fled the hospice for a few hours. We are alone in the hospice's comfy other wing. "My brother Mike. He was Dad's favorite."

"Is this recent?" I ask.

Suddenly the major plot point that opens my screenplay's third act comes into view. This is the complication that will propel us through to the thrilling climax. Suicide piled high with layers of regret. I'm not entitled to this family secret, but that hasn't stopped me so far.

"No," she rubs at her nose. "But I guess it still seems like it. He took pills. Dad found him. Said Mike looked like he was asleep in the middle of a great dream."

"Wow. Any warning?"

"Sure, if we'd been paying attention. Mike mailed us all notes that came a few days later. Creepy, but nice. He told me I was the most beautiful girl in the world. But then said he was no proper judge because the beauty of this life escaped him."

"I bet that destroyed your parents."

"Mom and Dad were close again at the funeral, but after that they never talked much. It was like it cemented their divorce. I was just finishing college and they both disappeared. Bob, too."

She sits next to me in profile, her lips parted and her eyelashes flickering. Suddenly I understand something. What I'd thought of as signs of a happy family are actually hints that they've adapted and now float around the tragedy like lifeboats around a sunken ship, each wave bumping them against the wreckage anew.

"I'm sorry," I say. "I can't imagine a worse moment."

"I wish I couldn't." Carla looks deep into the palm of her hand. ꕥ

THE DAUGHTER

AFTER THE ABORTION, CARLA couldn't stop thinking about Christmas trees.

She gripped the X–Acto knife and sliced into the green vinyl of the stool next to her, recreating the stair step pattern of a pine. Her editor, Arnulfo Saenz, had warned her about this habit, but lately she couldn't control the need to destroy things.

The holidays were a month away, and she wouldn't be able to leave this tiny Central Texas town and her six–month–old job as a newspaper reporter until at least the twenty–third. But that wasn't it. Christmas trees were how her family measured time. The trees were short and squat in every photograph, their branches guarding a mountain of shimmering toys that seemed to grow like a tumor in each successive year. When the grand unveiling time came, she and her brothers Mike and Bob would stake out different corners of the room to stack their piles of loot.

Carla finished cutting and eased the blade under her handiwork, lifting the small, vinyl Christmas tree gently from the stool's foam rubber insides and sliding it into her palm. She held it up to her face and sniffed.

Just then the door to the composing room swung open and the press foreman barged in.

Carla looked up at Dameron "Dam" Heitmiller's grin and flinched.

"Caught with your hand in the cookie jar," he said. "Saenz will can your ass if you're not careful, kid."

Dam was a muscular, fortyish man whose smirking eyes and slicked–back, thick hair made it always seem to Carla that he was laughing at her youth. There was no denying she looked a good five years younger than her actual twenty–three. She was the kind of thin, blonde, and cute that made her mother's friends defensive and her father's buddies goofy. Her only hope was to flirt back defiantly.

"Where's your Christmas spirit, Santa? A girl needs toys this time of year."

"I'll let that one pass."

He took the vinyl tree from her hand and pressed it into the hole it had left. Dam's ink–stained hands then reached for a roll of clear tape, ripped a strip free, and spread it across the area.

"Now, sorority, if you'd be so kind as to get this section laid out so I can put it to press. My ex is letting the kids have dinner with me tonight. Life is calling."

ꕥ ꕥ ꕥ

Life was calling Carla names. She was twenty–six hours removed from the abortion clinic and still ninety percent numb.

Yesterday morning she'd converted half of her meager paycheck to cash and driven the twenty miles back to her college campus to meet Brad, worrying along the way both that he wouldn't show and that the steady oil leak in her Honda would destroy the car.

She'd fed two quarts into the thirsty engine and dumped the plastic oil containers in the back seat where a dozen other empties waited. At stop lights the oil drenched the pavement in a steady flow.

Brad was home.

The apartment door opened to his sad eyes and half smile. Carla slipped her arms around his waist and squeezed tight. She led him to the bedroom and undressed him, laughing at the opportunity.

"This is going to be the safest sex you'll ever have, mister man," she said as she slipped out of her panties.

Carla pushed Brad onto the waterbed he'd inherited from his groovy seventies–generation dad and mounted him. The sex was good, angry, and fast. She imagined Brad's penis jabbing the baby's head. She slammed down harder and rode the waves.

An hour later she heard the whirr and felt the pull as the baby disintegrated. It and Brad's semen drained from her body as one.

ꕥ ꕥ ꕥ

For the past two months Saenz had given Carla the task of putting together the women's pages without his help. The section's front cover was their creative piece of the week. This time it was a photo essay about a Christmas party at an old folks' home. The inside was a slapdash of school lunch menus, weddings, and folksy society columns about who came a–calling at whose engagement party.

Most of the layout was done on computer, but the ads had to be constructed, rolled in melted wax, and pasted onto the page in the old school way. Carla went through the process on instinct and the thought made her smile. She had come to this job at the urging of a professor. The prof called it boot camp. Do a year, get the skills, move on. The end was in sight.

When her sorority sisters graduated and moved on to jobs at Austin computer companies and Dallas accounting firms, Carla descended into the sticks. She had no other option. Their parents were anxious to help; hers were nowhere to be found since her brother's death. Carla was determined to fly solo into the real world. Plus she loved newspapers, had loved them since high school when her takeoff of a gossip column got her expelled for three days for implying that Principal Harrison was wearing women's panties under that ugly polyester suit. The other kids laughed at her words and she basked in the notoriety.

She looked to her right and saw Saenz at the easel examining her handiwork. He was smiling. His basketball of a belly jiggled slightly as his pockmarked face nodded in approval.

"You're getting too professional," he said. "Soon you'll be hired off by a big daily and I'll be saying I knew you when."

"God, I can only hope." Carla noticed the whine in her voice and added a quick, "No offense."

"None taken."

Saenz was a good guy, she'd decided. At first he'd scared her with his deep frown lines and monotone voice. The best she could figure he was a sixties survivor who'd drunk it and drugged it, then mostly given it up.

"Listen," Saenz said, "I'm planning to get a Christmas tree tonight. Dam gave me directions to a place where I can chop down my own and it won't cost a cent. Want to come?"

Carla planted her hands at her hips and dropped her chin conspiratorially.

She deadpanned, "Why, sir, I'm not sure if you have designs to fraternize with me or if you simply desire an accomplice to your crime."

A deep red appeared on Saenz's neck and migrated to his cheeks. Carla couldn't resist toying with him, but it was too easy. Saenz was as closed off as he was kind.

"Sure," she said. "I'd like to get a tree. And the price is right. But right now I'm late for cops."

ഗ ഗ ഗ

The police station/jail was in a closed grocery store that had been painted a somber beige, its interior partitioned into cubicles much like the big–city newsrooms that Carla had dreamed of since seeing one in an old movie.

Among her duties was to meet once a week with the police chief, a skinny cowboy named Randall Posey whose breath reeked of mouthwash.

"Guess it's that time again," he said without quite looking up from his desk.

Were all men afraid to look a woman in the eyes?

"I'm like a drunken frat boy, chief," Carla said. "I come around once a week whether it's good for me or not."

Posey looked up at her finally, his eyes squinting.

"I expect you'll want to know about the murder."

It was the first she'd heard of it, but she nodded. "Murder–suicide, actually," he said and dropped the police report on the table in front of her. "College girl. About your age, I imagine. Caught the attention of a bad dude. Sometimes it's all a matter of luck turning the wrong direction."

A middle–aged woman with a bad perm came to the desk holding a CD. She looked at Carla and offered a tight–lipped grin.

"Should I show her the photos?"

The woman was thick around the middle and impatient. She reminded Carla of her mother's friends, the ones whose bodies had never quite sprung back from babies and who fought the years by dying their hair red.

"I don't believe that's necessary," Posey said. He raised his palm toward the woman as if halting an oncoming train.

"She might as well report the truth," she said. "Open people's eyes."

"Carla, this is Cindy Juricka, our CSI."

"Crime scene investigator. Not like on TV," Cindy said. "That's a load of crap. I just document the crime scene. You want to see?"

"Yes, please," Carla said. She felt like she'd just agreed to take communion in a strange church.

"Be kind now," the sheriff said.

The woman settled behind a computer at a nearby desk and brought up a slide show of photos.

"He'd been calling her," Cindy said. "Somehow got her pager number and her home phone. She came back Sunday night about dusk with a basket full of freshly washed laundry. He was waiting at her door. See the basket there?"

The photo showed the second–story entrance to an apartment like where Carla had lived for a time in college. The concrete was stained a dark purple next to the laundry.

"She tried to push the door shut, but he pulled out a pistol and shot. It went through the wood and in and out of the sides of her stomach. Ended up lodged in the table next to her bed."

Cindy clicked and brought up a photo of the girl's living room taken from the front doorway. To the right was a bar lined with plastic souvenir cups, the kind they give out for free at football games. The living room walls were covered with posters for rock bands that had been popular a few years ago.

"She worked with him," Cindy said.

Her eyes were hard, but Carla got the idea the woman was trying to teach her something.

"He dragged her into the bedroom, stripped off her clothes and raped her."

Cindy's words were so matter of fact that the next photo jolted Carla even more. The woman was on the bed, her face a mask of blood, her patch of pubic hair exposed. Carla felt guilty looking at the photo, like she was committing her own criminal act of indecency.

"When he was through, he shot her in the heart."

Cindy pointed to a small hole above the woman's breast.

"Why all the blood on her face?" Carla asked.

"That's his blood. When the SWAT team arrived, the asshole ate a bullet and dropped naked atop her."

"Where is he in the photos?"

Cindy's eyes narrowed.

"Officers had drug him off her before I got there. Bounced what was left of his head on the steps on the way down. Left a lot of blood. Can't blame them for taking out a little anger, but it sure made a mess."

The next photo pulled back slightly and showed the entire room. On the wall behind the bed was a painting of a big–eyed girl holding a puppy. It belonged in a child's room.

"What was her name?" Carla asked.

"It's all in the report," the officer said. "I believe they said her nickname was Peanut. Yeah, I couldn't forget that."

Carla nodded.

"I don't think I'll be able to forget it either," she said.

ɞɞɞ

The first time Carla entered her sorority house after graduation, they hinted that she should give a donation. In a few months she had gone from friend to Miss Money Bags. They'd already begun to speak a new language, and stared blankly when she called them "sneeches," last year's term for girls on the make. They gossiped about boys, parties, and clothes; she stifled a scream and a yawn came out instead.

Brad was always busy with the usual—intramural sports, keg parties, sometimes even studying. When they got together she found they had nothing to say, so they hopped into bed instead. It helped.

ɞɞɞ

Home for Carla was a small, white apartment in a cube of a complex five blocks from the newspaper office. She couldn't afford a bed so the bedroom became a huge closet. She slept on a foldout sofa that her mother had given her, pulled the comforter up over her nose and most nights, less lately, cried herself to sleep watching reruns on an ancient television. The actual bedroom housed the clothes she'd hoarded during the days when she had an employee discount at the outlet mall. She frowned at the scattered piles as she watched them quickly go out of style.

The worst was the silence. The neighbors were nice enough. Sometimes she watched videos with Sarita, a slightly overweight single mom who lived next door. They'd wait until her two boys were asleep, get out the junk food and laugh through the worst romance movie they could find. When Sarita was busy, Carla turned the television down low and dozed on the sofa bed as the whispered voices cradled her.

ꕥ ꕥ ꕥ

Saenz was waiting outside the newspaper office wearing a heavy jacket and clutching a can of beer when she arrived, but he wasn't alone. Dam the press foreman came out toting a chainsaw.

"About time, college."

"I thought you had plans," she said.

"I did. Bitch changed her mind. Said the boy had the flu. And, besides, I didn't have the right attitude. Horse shit."

Saenz's truck had a camper shell in the back where Dam placed the chainsaw and an ice chest full of beer. Carla sat in the middle of the cab between the two men. She could feel Dam's leg rubbing against hers, but when she looked up he was gazing out the half–open window, tapping his lit cigarette against the glass and watching the ash fly away.

"Where is this place?" she asked.

"Lost Pines," Dam said.

"Dam knows a spot there," Saenz said as he steered them into the darkness. "You know about the Lost Pines?"

"Just that it's supposed to be pretty out there," she said.

Dam snorted and flicked his cigarette butt into the wind.

"It's a small area of pine forest that got separated from the Piney Woods of East Texas by hundreds of miles," Saenz said. "Orphans."

"Freak of nature," Dam said. "But the trees are ripe for the picking. Got to take what you can."

They drove into an area of the county Carla had never explored, down bumpy county roads that rattled through the truck and into Carla's chest. Her body clenched as she bobbed between the two men.

"Tell me about your kids," she said to Dam, hoping to cut through the quiet.

"Three girls and one boy," Dam said. "Boy's a queer."

"He's only ten," Saenz said.

"Ten-year-old who plays with dolls," Dam said. "He's prettier than the girls."

"Prettier than me?"

Carla threw out the flirty words to get a rise from the older men. In her experience it usually worked.

Dam offered a throaty chuckle in reply.

"What do you think, rich girl?" he said.

"That couldn't be possible," Saenz said softly without taking his eyes off the road.

The sign ahead read Dyson's Christmas Tree Farm. They slowed to a stop at a locked gate.

"Don't you have to pay for those trees?" Carla asked.

"Not if they don't catch you," Dam said. "Saenz, get us a few more beers while I jimmy the lock."

Saenz shrugged at her. His nose was flushed red and Carla wondered how many beers he'd consumed before she'd arrived.

"If we get caught, I'll take all the blame," he said.

"Promise?"

"I'm there for my reporters. No worries."

Saenz wandered to the back of the truck, and Carla watched as the headlights illuminated Dam at the fence working the lock with a piece of wire. Peanut's blood–caked face flashed in her mind. It was a week in which Carla could feel the last bits of her innocence crumbling. Peanut, Carla's brother Mike, the baby. She needed a Christmas tree today more than anything.

"Got it!"

Dam held the open lock up over his head and the headlights glinted off of the metal.

ꕥ ꕥ ꕥ

They drove slowly down the gravel road with the headlights off. Dam leaned out of the window, shining a flashlight in their path. All Carla could see of him were his tight faded jeans and muddy boots. From this angle his muscular legs could pass for those of a frat boy.

"Just a little farther." Dam's voice was muffled in the wind. "Here! Stop!"

Carla stepped out into the cool air while the men did their work. Saenz held the first tree while Dam cut. When the tree fell, Saenz tumbled to the ground, too. He stayed flat on his back, giggling.

"Boy's past his limit," Dam said. "Help me get him in the truck."

They lifted Saenz by his armpits and half guided, half carried him to the truck's cab.

"Be a good boy, Dam," he slurred as they rolled him in.

"If you can't be good, be good enough," Dam said.

Carla took Saenz's job and held the next tree while Dam silently positioned the chainsaw. When it started to cut, Carla could feel the motor vibrating deep into her body. She held tighter and tried to empty her mind. It almost worked.

The tree dropped from her hands to the ground and Dam side-stepped it as he rose to his feet. He looked deep into Carla's eyes and held the stare for what she realized was a moment too long.

"Not bad for the idle rich," he said. "Two down and one to go."

"I choose the last one."

Carla folded her hands at her chest and gave her best tough guy look.

"Choose away," Dam said. "Never met a woman yet who didn't have to have it her way."

He went to the back of the truck and sunk his hand into the ice chest. It emerged wet and ruddy with a fresh can of beer.

She walked among the nearby trees, sizing them up, remembering the Christmas tree lots of her youth. She could smell the freshly baked gingersnaps and taste the eggnog her family enjoyed while decorating the tree. Her Dad and brother Mike argued as they tried to unravel the lights they'd left in a tangled mess the year before. Bob blew tinsel to the upper branches.

"That one."

The pine was fat but not too tall, it's bottom full and devoid of any empty patches.

Dam held up the chainsaw and saluted the tree with it.

"Its time has come," he said.

As he squatted to the tree, Dam steadied his hand on Carla's waist then skimmed it along her jeans. Her body tensed, but she did not look at him. She would not give him the satisfaction.

The cutting seemed quicker to her this time. Dam slashed at the tree and it fell before she could stop it. He took twine and spiraled it around each of the three trees to pull their branches in tight for the ride home.

Carla was anxious to get away, to be in her apartment and for the first time in her life to decorate a tree solo. She remembered as a child on the beach trying to pick up one grain of sand. But it was impossible as the sand always clumped together. Today she was a grain of sand on a giant beach and she refused to be sad. Store–bought cookies and eggnog. She'd consume them and fall asleep under the glow of the tree she herself chose.

"Grab the front."

Dam pointed at a bound tree.

She grasped the top and walked it toward the truck's camper. She couldn't see Dam behind her as they eased it onto the truck bed. She let go and Dam slid it forward, thrusting close to her back.

She turned and his mouth was there, reeking of angry beer. He moved his mouth toward hers, but she twisted her face away.

"A little tiger," he whispered in her ear.

He wrapped his arms around her waist and she could feel his hardness grinding at her.

"No."

As she said the word, she knew it was too little too late. Saenz was passed out. It would be Dam's word against hers.

She turned to find his eyes, to plead with him.

"Christmas."

It was the only word she could come up with. She would not cry.

"You got a present for me, college girl?"

He reached down and unsnapped her jeans. His rank breath found her neck. Carla tried to tear away, but it was no use. OhGodOhGodOhGod. A grain of sand. He jabbed his hand down into her panties and his fingers were like worms invading her.

But Dam jerked back. His hand came free, and she dropped to her knees and began to sob. She looked up and Dam was holding his hand to his face and grimacing.

"On the fucking rag!"

He poured the rest of his beer over the hand and grabbed a fresh one from the ice chest.

"I do not swim in the Red Sea, little girl."

"Fuck you!" she screamed.

"Not tonight."

He lifted her from the ground and shoved her into the truck bed next to the Christmas tree. The other two trees quickly took their places around her.

"I got a little overboard." Dam would not look at her. "Let's keep this to ourselves."

As he slammed the hatch, Carla knew she had no choice. She had no more say than the freshly cut trees that rested around her. Soon she'd leave this town and never tell anyone about tonight. She'd grow warier and stronger, and always be on guard. She could never rely on anyone again. The utter isolation of this new truth left her numb.

But she knew she was luckier than Peanut, or Mike, or the baby. The blood and the sanitary napkin that had alerted Dam to it was from the abortion. One disaster averted another. This for that. Her lost baby had saved her. As the truck swayed down the road and the cool air flowed by, Carla listened to the slosh of the frigid water in the ice chest and let the Christmas trees rub up against her skin. She imagined she was one of them: freshly cut, alone, and moving with every bump in the road that took her farther from home. ☙

THE SCREENWRITER

"I SAW YOUNG MEN dressed in white," Mr. Wright says.

"Was this a dream?" I say.

"No. They were standing right behind you there. One fellow lolling on the windowsill. Last night. They were waiting for me. Not too impatiently, thank God. What's really odd is I recognized one of the chaps."

"An angel?"

"It was my son Mike."

Mr. Wright looks at once pleased and bewildered by his own statement. His two living children have left for dinner, left us to make sense of his life.

"Carla told me you found your son's body."

"Horrible, horrible moment…"

He caresses the pocket angel I gave him yesterday. At Mr. Wright's request, Carla had taken it to a jeweler and had a hoop attached so her father can wear it around his neck.

"My son, my beautiful boy, had an affliction, Matt. Or at least he believed he did. He was terminally sad. He told me once that he couldn't love, that he was wired wrong."

"I can't imagine opening up like that to my father," I say.

"Mike and I connected," he says. "My other kids wouldn't fess up to anything. Bob's moody, Carla's independent and headstrong. Mike was a jock and, like me, an artistic soul."

"What did he do for a living?"

I'm doing it again, I think, picking at someone's scabs, digging for truth.

"Ah, the big question: what do you do? We Americans define ourselves by profession. I'm no different. Mike was a guitar god, an axe slinger. The women adored him, even as he pushed them away. Even more as he pushed them away! A whole gaggle of ga–ga geese at the funeral. Unloved? No. Unable to love? Perhaps."

"Did you blame yourself when he died?" I ask.

His eyelids close and he is quiet for a moment.

"I wasn't there for the tough times," Mr. Wright says. "I was too busy erecting edifices to my own ego. Damn right, I blamed myself.

My old man was too testosterone–addled to show feelings. I vowed to not be that guy. I tried. I told my kids I loved them."

His eyes open and he turns to look at me.

"Darkness. A pit. That's where I dwelled. I gave some thought to taking my own life, something I'd never come close to before, not even after the divorce."

"How'd you snap out of it?"

"Janice."

"So you fell in love."

"With a younger woman." Mr. Wright winks. "Barely out of college, God help me. She was Mike's girlfriend."

"Wow."

"Shock you? Did me, too. She was beautiful and wild. Kinky hair one step removed from an Afro. Olive skin and the saddest eyes I'd ever seen.

"It started innocently enough, but grief mixed with lust. In some perverse manner we were the perfect fit. She made me feel young. I wasn't the geezer I am now, but I was well into the kingdom of the old fart. And she saw echoes of Mike in me. We'd huddle under the covers and tell stories about my boy.

"The passion was intense. She'd show up wearing nothing but a trench coat. We did it on my office desk, in fields of flowers, on the steps of the state capitol. All the fun stuff that seems so naughty."

"What happened to her?" I ask.

"She was young enough to think it was love. Started talking about marriage and kids. My ex wife and the kids found out and got *pissed*. Then Janice and I got a dog…"

Mr. Wright's words get lost in a fit of coughs and his face begins to turn a light purple. He points at a plastic glass on a nearby table. I grab it, hold the straw to his lips, and watch him drink. Slowly a very pale pink returns to his skin.

"Where was I?"

"The dog."

"Yes, Elmo the dog. Our practice baby. Janice named the pound puppy. A little cocker spaniel with ears we couldn't resist. We were shacking up at her little second–floor pad in a monster of an apartment complex off the interstate. The neighbor was a black militant whose rap music knifed through us at all hours. I responded by cranking up a little Bach and facing the speakers toward the wall. We'd escape the racket by walking the dog. In my deluded mind we were a young couple pampering the pooch. But we strolled a war zone, and I was a dirty old man.

"Janice had a degree in art and hustled up a graphic design job with one of the state agencies. Strictly nine to five. I had to get back to work, too, so Elmo resided on the balcony during the day. Not a pretty sight!"

"A little dog poop problem?" I ask.

"Not a little, a lot. That pooch could produce. And the pee leaked down below on the neighbors who may or may not have been armed. We finally had to nail up a kiddy barrier and house him in the kitchen. It was a small improvement.

"But, frankly, Janice was wising up about me as mate material. I proved a poor imitation of Mike. And the worst? The dog hated her. Loved me; hated her.

"I was spending more and more nights on a cot at the office. One night she rang me there and said Elmo had flown the coop. She'd come home with a load of groceries, opened the doggie gate, and Elmo darted out the open door. He never looked back.

"I went over there and we searched for him, but I could tell her heart wasn't in it. We ended up in the sack. The balling was mechanical. I remember staring up at the ceiling afterward in silence feeling totally and completely alone. That's when I finally accepted Mike was gone, and Janice and I had to get on with living."

"So you never found Elmo," I say.

"Never. Macho man that I was I gave it the old college try later that night. Drove around the complex looking like an undercover narc. A guy with a mohawk sneered at me. And there were cats everywhere! On car hoods. Strolling the driveway. Sitting about having cat parties. Not a dog in sight."

"Any idea what became of Janice?"

"Married, got fat, had two point five kids and lives in the suburbs last I heard. Probably has a pet cat. I get Christmas cards from her. She signs her name but doesn't include a note. I don't think she wants to be reminded of failing at love with both the son and the father. But I owe her. Because of Janice I was able to accept my culpability in Mike's death and get on with it. I forgave myself for being an asshole. Mea culpa! Mea culpa!"

"So what was the best moment of your life?"

I can't help myself. I want to know more.

"Best moment?"

A stocky man enters carrying a food tray. His hair is gray at the temples, but his face is childlike.

"Clyde!"

"Pasta fagioli, Charlie," he says. "Just like you ordered."

"Matt, meet the chef," Mr. Wright says. "Whatever a dying fool can imagine, Clyde can whip up. If anything can restore my appetite his sorcery can."

"You're too kind," Clyde says and lifts the lid on the soup. "Now try and eat a bit."

Mr. Wright takes a long sniff.

"Heaven," he says. "I'll give it a go. Say, my compadre here wants to know the best moment of my life. I'm coming up dry. Got anything I can steal?"

Clyde rubs at his chin. His eyes are friendly slits.

"Did you know I lived in Colorado for a few years after my parents split? My mother remarried."

"A divorce story! God help us," Mr. Wright says. "Quit blaming the old fogies. We did the best we could, kiddoes."

"No, not a sad story," Clyde says. "Though my stepfather did die a few years later. An accident at work. We moved back here to Texas and I never went back. But I only tell stories to lift your spirits, Charlie."

"Out with it, son," Mr. Wright says. "We're overdue."

"Do you remember when men landed on the moon?" Clyde says. "I was in the second grade." ☙

THE COOK

BILLY AND SAM WERE at the door about the time I finished the sweet, brown milk left over from my Apple Jacks. That was my favorite part. I had to eat six whole boxes to get the bowl. It looks like an apple somebody cut in half.

Grabbed my notebook and out the door.

"Hey, Clyde, get your coat and let's slide," Sam said with a giggle.

It was hard to get used to the cold. I didn't ever see snow till we moved to Denver. Mom had just packed up the station wagon and we left Texas. Dad stayed behind, but he came up sometimes and we stayed in a hotel and ate hot fudge sundaes. My brother Ethan—he was big, he was in the sixth grade and tried to tell me what to do—said it was called divorce. He said nobody really liked anybody after awhile. I knew Ethan sure got on my nerves a lot.

My coat was all folded up on the couch with my lunch sitting in a paper bag on top of it. I ran out the door and put my coat on at the same time.

Ice!

"We won't be late today. We can pretend we're in the Olympics. On your mark," Sam said, crouching low.

"They're off," I said as Billy and Sam skidded down the shiny concrete, the rubber of their galoshes squeaking.

"Russia's in the lead, but, wait, his skates are locking up. America's coming on strong. An elbow to the ribs. Did the officials see it? No! America hits the finish line. Another gold medal for Kowalski!"

Billy rolled on the frozen grass. "Hey, no fair. And how come I'm always Russia? I want to be Australia. I'll be a kangaroo and hop to the finish line."

"There's no ice in Australia, dummy," Sam said. "That's down at the equator and they swim all year long."

We slid down the sidewalk, stopping to crack off hunks of ice with our galoshes. These guys were okay. They were only in the first grade, but Sam had a pool table in his basement. It took his dad an hour once to get Billy's arm out of one of the ball–catching holes. Billy didn't scream, but he wouldn't play pool anymore.

I was in the second grade, so I had to be the leader. I beat Sam up one time when he said he wanted to push the button to let us cross Morton Street. He ran home crying and I hid out back by the incinerator until Mom called me in for supper. We had squash, but I ate it anyway.

Sam didn't complain this time when we got to Morton Street. You had to push the button and make it say WALK. Sam and Billy weren't through learning how to read yet, so I had to push the button. Mrs. Brinkman said I could move up to the green readers next.

One time we'd seen a man on the street next to a motorcycle. He was bleeding and everything. Billy's brother had a motorcycle. He was in high school and dated girls.

I couldn't wait to get to school and see Collette. She was kind of my girlfriend, only we didn't date or anything. Collette had long blond hair and freckles right across her nose. Perfect freckles. She was tall, too.

I told my brother—that's Ethan, we share a room. I told Ethan that Collette and me were going to get married and we'd even live in the same house. He laughed and shook his head. I wouldn't tell Ethan that her name was Collette, but I said her last name was White. He said he knew her brother and that only dummies get married.

"Guys, come quick!" Billy yelled from down at Fowser Street. He maybe could make the Olympics as fast as he slid down there.

"Wow, it's a quarter," Sam said. "We could go down to the 7–Eleven and buy some Monkees bubble gum cards."

"My Mom says they're hippies," I said.

"It's mine. I saw it first." Billy looked like that time Sam talked him into spending his birthday money on comic books and Sam borrowed them for a week. Sam spilled Coke all over Spiderman and the pages got all stuck together.

"Well, pick it up then," Sam said with that grin you knew meant trouble.

I pushed past Sam and saw. The quarter was on the sidewalk all right. It was a shiny, new 1970. Problem was there was a bunch of ice between it and Billy. Sam laughed so hard he had to sit down. Billy kicked the ice with his heel. It just turned white and crinkly.

Here it was. Sam would make Billy cry and we'd never get that quarter. But I turned my head and Sam was just sitting there talking to himself.

"Clyde, how come your Mom put your name on the outside of your coat?"

"Huh?"

"Says so right there. Clyde la… Clyde lo…"

I tore that coat right off my back. I didn't care how cold it was. "Clyde loves Collette," it said in thick marks like from those fat pencils we used before we were big kids. Sometimes I wished I had a time machine. I'd go way back to when my brother was a little bitty kid and beat him up. And I'd tell him if he didn't leave his little brother alone, I'd come back and make him go to school in nothing but his underwear.

"We'd better get to school or else we'll be late," I told Sam and Billy instead.

"Aren't you going to put your jacket on?"

"What about my quarter? School's only two blocks away. We've got time."

"My Mom says if you don't wear your coat the cold gets inside you and you have to stay home until it gets out."

"I like to get sick. I watch TV all day and Dad brings me comic books when he comes home for lunch. Is that what you're trying to do, Clyde?"

"I'm trying to not be late for school. Quit being such a baby."

Billy hung his head low. He didn't like being called a baby. His sister used to make him be the baby when she played Mommy and Daddy with her friends. Sam found out and told all the little kids in first grade.

My fingers were feeling funny by the time our feet hit the crunchy gravel by the monkey bars. Sam and Billy walked on to the third house. They called them cottages, but they were really just houses. I went to school in the second one with the big kids. The first one was where the principal, Mrs. Whitehead, lived. You didn't want to go in there.

Richard asked why I was shaking so much when I sat down on the bench to pull off my galoshes. He called them rubbers. Richard could run fast. He got a blue ribbon at Field Day last year. I got a white one, but it wasn't in the same race as Richard.

Mrs. Brinkman looked at me kind of funny when I opened my desk and pushed my coat in there all wadded up, but she didn't say anything about hanging it up in the hall.

It was an okay morning. We had to do arithmetic, but I didn't get called up to the chalkboard. John Peebles did and he got real embarrassed because he didn't do his homework. He turned red and most everybody laughed. Collette didn't laugh. I didn't either.

Mrs. Brinkman said we'd have a big surprise after recess. Mr. Yancy the janitor wheeled in a TV real slow. Mr. Yancy was old and he couldn't hear good. Sometimes we yelled at him, but he just smiled and waved. Nobody yelled this time. We were going to watch TV and see the astronauts.

Richard told Mrs. Brinkman that his Dad said it was a waste of money to send people to the moon again and again when there were people starving everywhere.

"My Dad said we already beat the commies there, so what's the big deal anyway?" Richard said. "He said they just walk around collecting a bunch of stupid rocks."

Mrs. Brinkman nodded her head and looked real serious. Sometimes I thought she was maybe the smartest lady ever.

"When I was a little girl, my parents would have laughed at the thought of going to the moon or exploring the stars," she said. "I guess what we don't understand is exciting to some people and a waste of time to others. I'm just sorry they took so long to get to the moon. I'm afraid it's too late for me. Maybe that's for the best. My students on the moon would float right out the window when they got bored."

We all laughed and Mrs. Brinkman quit being so serious.

"Now, who here would like the chance to go to the moon themselves one day?" she asked.

Everybody raised their hands, even Richard.

"Well, you can do anything you put your minds to," she said. "You'd better watch closely today to see what's in store for you. Recess for ten minutes and hurry back to your seats so you don't miss a thing."

Everybody else ran for the door, but I took my time getting up and peeked inside my desk to see if my coat was okay. I went over and told

Mr. Yancy I'd help him with the TV, but he smiled and said he was doing fine. Richard brought his Matchbox cars and said he would let me play with them if I didn't get them all dirty. I told him I was going to stay by the door in case Mr. Yancy needed help. Mrs. Brinkman looked at me from way over at her desk. I was going to tell her I tore my coat, but I was afraid she'd want to fix it, so I just pushed on the door and went outside.

It was windy in my face, so I crept along the wall to in between the buildings. The bricks felt warm on my back, but I had to wrap my arms tight to keep my front from freezing.

"What are you staring at?" Mary Rogers asked, looking me up and down. "You're weird, Clyde Bergman."

She was holding one end of a jump rope, Betty Roemer had the other end, and a bunch of girls were standing in line waiting to bounce up and down for a while. Mary Rogers started saying something about falling out of a tree and they counted, "Doctor one, doctor two, doctor three," while Suzie Plimpton jumped.

Collette was next and she looked at me and smiled funny.

"Wake up, Collette. It's your turn," Mary Rogers said and stuck her tongue out at me. It was all white and looked like a snail when you pull it out of its shell.

My fingers felt like they were turning purple. I tucked them into my sweater. Collette's hair floated and her skirt went way up. Mary Rogers said, "Cinder–ella had a fell–a …"

The most perfect freckles ever. My feet were tingly and my head felt funny. I didn't know how many times she jumped up in the air. I was trying to listen for the number when Mrs. Brinkman grabbed my arm and said the astronauts were about to land on the moon.

ᔓ ᔓ ᔓ

My brother Ethan got this model of the space ship for his birthday from my Dad. We'd stayed in the hotel with my Dad a whole weekend. My Dad said maybe Ethan could be an astronaut when he grew up, but Ethan said he wanted to be a lawyer. My Dad laughed and asked who Ethan'd work for, him or Mom. Ethan got mad, but he built the model anyway. It was not the whole ship or anything. It was just the part that lands on the moon, with legs on it like on a spider. There was a little bitty astronaut that stood next to it on this little bitty piece of moon. He was all alone holding this flag in the middle of a bumpy nowhere. Ethan said I couldn't touch his model because I'd break it, but sometimes when he was not around I did anyway.

By the time we sat down at our desks, I was pretty much warmed up. The TV showed the moon out of the window of the space ship, just like how the astronauts were seeing it. Mrs. Brinkman didn't even have to tell us to shut up. Everybody had their mouths hanging open and their eyes wide, even Collette, only it didn't look so funny on her. The TV picture bounced up and down when they hit the moon and the TV man said, "Touchdown," just like in football.

Mrs. Brinkman turned the sound off on the TV and said we could keep on watching, but we had to get our English done. We got a test back. It had a bunch of questions and you had to say yes or no to them. Some were silly like, "Would a pear wear a hat?" or "Can an owl growl?" Both are no, of course. The only one I missed was, "Would it be a good trick to put a brick on a glass?" I said the answer was yes, but Mrs. Brinkman marked it wrong. I'd still like to see it. My brother Ethan and his friends put a bunch of my Mom's glasses on top of a fence one time and shot them with a BB gun. Ethan got grounded for a week. He's always doing crazy stuff like that and getting in trouble. Ethan wouldn't let me touch the gun and it wasn't even his.

On the other side of the fence behind our house was this highway, but there was a place before you got to it that was all dirt. Ethan and his friends worked for about a month digging this big hole out there. They got a bunch of boards from the dump and nailed them together to cover the hole up, and they pushed dirt on top of the boards so you could hardly tell it was there. The hole was so deep I could stand up in it. I helped them dig it, but then Ethan said it was only for big kids. I didn't want to play in their crummy hole anyway.

A couple of weeks later these men came in a big truck and filled the hole up. Ethan got grounded again. My friend Sam heard somebody say this girl who lived down the street—she was in fifth grade and had this blue stuff over her eyes—went in the hole with Ethan's friends and took off her underwear while they watched with a flashlight. I said I didn't know what the big deal was. I saw my Mom's friend put a diaper on this little girl baby once, and there's nothing down there to see. I thought it was weird, but I didn't say anything to my Mom. I asked

Ethan, but he got mad and told me to keep my big, fat mouth shut. Sometimes I think Ethan is right about nobody really liking anybody.

The astronauts were almost ready to come out, so we stayed inside at lunch and ate at our desks. Usually we could go outside if we wanted to after they brought the milk cartons up from the basement on big trays. Next year we would be in the big school and they'd have a cafeteria so we wouldn't have to bring our sandwiches with us. My sandwich was bologna with mustard. Suzie Plimpton passed out the milk, and she whispered in my ear, "Collette likes you," and walked away real quick. I looked over at Collette, but she wouldn't look back. Mary Rogers and her goofy friends started laughing. My face got real warm. Mrs. Brinkman told everybody to be quiet and turned the TV up. One astronaut was already on the moon, and he was setting up a TV camera so we could see the other guy come down the ladder. It was like he was pushing himself down instead of falling down. He stepped on the moon and we all clapped like crazy.

You could tell that walking on the moon wasn't like walking on the earth. Everything was real slow. It looked fun, but weird, too. The astronauts had to kind of hop, and if they hopped too much they went way up in the air and it took a long time for them to come down. I could jump higher than just about anybody when we played basketball, but not that high.

The day was almost over, but Mrs. Brinkman said she wanted us to draw a picture and write a story to go with it before we went home. She said it could be about the astronauts or anything we wanted, but we had to read it in class the next day. I tried to think of something Collette would like, but I couldn't think of anything. I finally drew a picture of a horse and wrote, "My Ranch Visit. One summer I visited my uncle's ranch. One day we rode over a hill and saw a green horse with blue spots." Richard saw my picture and said it looked like a dog. He drew the moon.

When Mrs. Brinkman said we could go, I acted like I was putting my books in my desk until most everybody was gone. I pulled my coat out and folded it so nobody could read it and went to get my galoshes. Sam and Billy got out early with the other little kids and sometimes they waited for me outside, but they were already gone when I went back out into the cold. The playground was empty.

I went over the gravel and saw Collette carrying a notebook and walking real slow on the other side of the street from me. I walked faster, but not too fast. Collette was wearing a blue coat and a little blue cap. She lived about three blocks from me. I knew because Billy and Sam and me used to play with a guy who lived over there. He had about a million pieces of Lego.

For about two blocks Collette and me walked right across from each other. She looked over and smiled at me one time. Right before Morton Street I crossed over to where Collette was at the crosswalk. It's a really busy street.

"You want me to push the button?" I said.

"No, thanks, I already did," she said. Collette had shiny blue eyes.

When it said WALK, we went across at the same time. The sun was shining and most of the ice was water again, but it was still pretty cold.

"Did you like the astronauts?" I said, just to say something.

"Yes."

"I want to go to the moon like Mrs. Brinkman said."

Collette looked in my eyes. "Wouldn't you be scared up there all alone? I'd be lonely."

"I don't know. Maybe. Want me to carry your book?"

"Okay."

Collette gave me the book and then stuck out her hand. It was covered with a fat, red mitten. I held it anyway.

"Is your dad a cowboy in Texas?"

"No," I said. "He wears a tie and goes to an office downtown."

"My stepfather has a store. What does your stepfather do?"

"I don't have a stepfather yet, just a jerky brother," I said.

"Oh. My sister's mean, too." Collette stared at my shirt. "Aren't you cold without your coat?"

"Yeah," I said and smiled. I put the books down for a second and put my jacket on. It was warm. I held Collette's hand again and thought of the astronauts in those big, shiny suits. They didn't know much about the moon except that it doesn't have air. Maybe they were scared, but I bet it was fun goofing around in those suits.

I squeezed Collette's hand and wondered how high Collette and me would float if we jumped straight up in the air. ☙

THE SCREENWRITER

"WOMEN AND THE COSMOS, the two great mysteries of life," Mr. Wright says. "I've never figured out either."

The soup sits untouched and Mr. Wright's face has turned a chalky hue.

"Clyde, lean in that little fridge and rescue the miss, kiss, something." The words trail off. "The goddamned bottle."

Clyde pulls out a bottle of whiskey.

"You want this jigger?" he asks.

"Yeah, my souvenir of the late, great Astrodome," Mr. Wright says. "Fill her up."

Clyde empties the jigger down Mr. Wright's throat and the old man sits back smiling as if he's just received communion.

"That's the ticket. Thanks for the touching tale, but you'd better call the nurse in here on your way out. I'm in need of better painkillers than booze."

"No problem," Clyde says. "Have your pal here microwave the soup when you're ready for it."

"Aces," Mr. Wright says.

Despite his pallor, Mr. Wright's eyes remain bright.

"A silly love story," he says when the chef is out of earshot. "But I can relate a bit. Greatest moment of my life? Maybe grabbing hold of the rope swing out front of my grandmother's East Texas farm. Fields and fields of sugar cane. Taking baths out back in a metal tub. Chasing the chickens. Being a boy with endless possibilities. No, it would be when my parents and I rode a steamer down the mighty Mississippi. I felt like Huck Finn lighting out for the territories!

"Women were my biggest failure, Matt. I was too busy at the job and too quick to pull it out of my pants. Never could hold on to a relationship for long."

"Did you remarry?" I ask.

"Sure. Twice. Nothing took. The kids' mother was the best, but she couldn't forgive me. I don't blame her. But we all die alone."

"You feeling OK?"

"No. Decidedly not. I'm considering leaving tonight, son. Got my bags packed for the final journey."

I don't know what to say.

Mr. Wright sniffs at the cold soup and curls his lip.

"Damn stuff tastes like paste. Everything does now. Fine last meal for a man. Get me some burgers!"

"I'll see what I can do," I say.

"God bless you, boy. I've never figured out God either, by the way." He grabs the spoon and stirs the soup.

"Do you believe?"

I point at the picture of Jesus.

"He was actually a stocky black man with short hair," Mr. Wright says.

"I've never heard that."

"This choir boy face is beautiful, but it's all marketing for the white masses. Yes, I suppose I believe in the Golden Rule and beautiful sunsets. But churches can go to hell. Too much social control, not enough contemplation. Am I offending you?"

"Hard to do," I say. "I've scarcely been in a church. My parents didn't take to them much either."

"Another heathen," he says. "Welcome to the cult. I asked the big questions when I was twelve and nobody could answer them: 'How can the universe have no end, and if God created everything, then who created him?'"

"I guess it's too much for our human minds to understand," I say.

"Bingo," Mr. Wright says. "We're not high enough on the brain chain to compute the big answers. Somewhere in the lack of an answer, that's where God truly resides."

"Then you do believe?"

"Yeah, Matt, I believe. There's an architecture term, interior spaciousness. That's what the higher power brings to us. But I'm getting too preachy."

I'm about to tell him to go on, when the male nurse comes in. He pulls back the covers and begins to massage Mr. Wright's feet. There are dark splotches on the old man's calves.

Mr. Wright looks at me and rolls his eyes.

"Marco's a bigger flirt than the girls."

"So you're having some pain?" the nurse says.

"Yeah. Hell of a way to leave this world."

I see my cue to go and wave on my way toward the door.

"Cheeseburgers! Two of them," Mr. Wright says. "Dripping with grease to perfection."

"Done," I say.

ꙮ ꙮ ꙮ

I check behind the counter and see the baby has died. The board is now filled with names of people I haven't met, have no desire to meet. In the middle is Mr. Wright. At any moment he will be erased and someone else will take his room. That's it. Death. The cold hard facts and there's not a damn thing we can do about it.

Marco walks up and smiles at me with a bit less wariness.

"Where are you going to get this perfect cheeseburger?"

"I know a place," I say.

"Get me one, too. No onions."

I nod.

"Why were you touching his feet?" I ask.

"Looking at the color mostly. But as the body begins to shut down, the feet get colder, circulation slows."

"If you don't mind me asking," I say, "where are the doctors?"

"Doctors prescribe the pain pills," Marco says and pats me on the shoulder. "They're around when needed. This isn't a hospital."

"So Mr. Wright's near the end?"

"Yes. He's asleep now. He's sliding back and forth between here and the beyond. And it is good you are here on this side for him. He thinks your writing is his immortality."

Just then Carla comes up behind me gripping something greenish brown. Her eyes widen when she sees us.

"I hope it's OK," she says and keeps going before we can answer.

Bob has the bottom of the Christmas tree, which is fully decorated with ornaments, lights, and tinsel. Pine needles litter their pathway.

Marco looks at me, at the tree disappearing down the hallway, and then back at me. We both start laughing.

"The kids are becoming the parents," Marco says. "I can relate."

THE MALE NURSE

"GRANDMAMA CALLED LAST NIGHT from Heaven," Marina said. "She asked how you were."

Marina was my older sister by three years. She was only sixteen, but Mama said Marina is older than anybody, at least since Grandmama died. Every morning Marina crawled into my bed when my eyes were crusty with sleep and told me dreams.

"It was so real, Marco," Marina said, her dark eyes wide. "Grandmama called from a pay phone. I could hear this other lady with a Yankee accent behind her telling Grandmama to hurry up, and dogs were barking."

Marina's lips turned down and her whole face tightened. "I said, 'Grandmama, do you know where you are? Do you know you've been dead to our Texas home for five years?' Grandmama didn't say anything, then she said, 'Oh, that explains a lot.'

"When I asked about Heaven she wouldn't answer. 'I really must hurry, Marina,' Grandmama said. 'There are people waiting.' She whispered with the other woman for a second and they both laughed. And she said, 'Tell Marco to take out the garbage and not get into fights at school.'"

I asked Marina, "Did she say anything about Mama?"

Marina smiled and leaned back on the bed. "I told Grandmama that Mama didn't mean anything when she called her a fat, old cow. I said, 'Mama was just being Mama and she was mad that she couldn't go dancing because you wouldn't stay home from bingo and baby–sit us.'

"Grandmama clicked her tongue. 'I'm not mad. My daughter–in–law is a foolish little girl, so different from you. That clock radio was awful pretty, though.'"

Grandmama won a clock radio at bingo but it was broke up when the drunk cab driver sent Grandmama sailing through the sky and left the stuff from her purse, radio dials, and plastic slivers scattered like confetti. At least that was what Marina told me.

"What else did Grandmama say?" I asked. I was finally starting to wake up.

"She said, 'Take care of everybody. They think they can't make it without you. And I'll see you real soon, Marina.' Then she hung up."

Marina put her hands behind her head and closed her eyes. Telling me dreams seemed to suck the life out of her. Her face lost color and her hands began to shake. I let her sleep and went and tried to make breakfast for Mama. Mama was born in Greece. Marina said Mama's parents brought her to South Texas to tame her and keep the wild boys away, but it didn't help. Papa came from Mexico. He left home for adventure. Papa said Greeks and Mexicans go together everywhere except in the kitchen. Mama's tortillas were fat and fell apart. Marina did the cooking and cleaned the house.

Mama built fancy doll houses and sold them to rich people. She worked on a bunch at one time because that way she didn't get bored. Once a month Marina and I had to finish them so Mama could pay the rent. Papa played accordion in a Tejano band, but he only lived here sometimes and his pay shrank on the way home. Most of the time he was on the road squeezing out notes. While he was gone, Mama went to dances most every night. She said her feet couldn't stay still. When Papa returned, he and Mama didn't leave their room. Sometimes they yelled at each other, but mostly they pinched each other for fun.

"Your Papa thinks I'm his instrument and he can squeeze me any time he wants," Mama would say and then wink. "He doesn't know who is really conducting this orchestra."

Papa was crazy about Marina. Last year he had worked extra hard so he could save enough money to throw Marina a party for her quinceañera. This was a party for when a girl becomes a woman. Mama said it was a stupid idea. Mama said she was too young to have a grown daughter. Papa laughed and kissed her behind the ear.

"Everybody will know that my Marina has become a woman. There will be a mass with candles and a party without end. I will invite the whole town to get fat off the finest meats and crazy drunk from the coldest beer," Papa said.

We didn't see Papa for a month, and, when he did show up, all he did was sleep. Marina said he played his squeezebox in bars as far away as Louisiana to save up for her party. Mama bought bright white and pink cloth to make a fancy dress. Then she sewed fringe and bells on.

It shined and jangled like something you might see on TV, only one of the sleeves was longer than the other. Marina had to straighten it out.

Marina was always in the kitchen. Grandmama taught Marina to cook, but she never could interest Mama in anything Mexican except Papa and dances.

"It's because Mama got married so young," Marina said. "She and Papa didn't get to be teenagers, so now that they're getting old they're trying to make up for it."

Marina understood everything, and it was hard to get her mad. During the plans for the party, she was all little–kid laughter one minute and tired sighs the next.

The morning of the quinceañera, Papa was one big grin, and Mama was holding his hand. The priest was waiting, the dress was made, the house smelled of chiles and chocolate, and the dance hall was full of colored streamers.

Everyone was invited. Papa patted his cheeks and said, "My little girl is a woman. Soon I will be an old man."

Mama cleared her throat and kicked him.

"Marina is the only one allowed to get old in this house," she said. "I'm not going to stay married to any old man who is full of worries."

Then Marina walked slowly, carefully down the stairs in the dress Mama had made. She looked like an angel. Only during the night her hair had turned as white as a cloud that holds no rain.

ᔕ ᔕ ᔕ

"I flew up to the treetops and held on there," Marina said. Marina flew a lot in her dreams.

"The leaves were soft in my hand. I could see our house below—you need to patch the roof, Marco. Then I let go and stretched my arms above my head like Supergirl. Papa was playing his squeezebox somewhere and I could see the notes. I flew sideways and plucked them from the air, one by one and ate them."

I asked, "What did they taste like?"

"I got one bad one that tasted like okra. I was flying faster and faster, passing cars on the highway heading for San Antonio. Then I saw something shining by the side of the road and swooped down to get a closer look.

"It was a suitcase made of the finest leather. I opened it and found a stuffed bear, a bicycle, a puppy, three baseballs, a spinning top, earrings made of gold, and fifty toy soldiers fighting over a flag. I scratched under the puppy's chin and closed the bag tight. With the handle sagging in my hands I could only fly about two feet off the road, so I dropped down and decided to walk home. I walked for hours and the bag got heavier and heavier. One of the soldiers shot a hole in the bag and the bullet bounced off my shin. See the scar? I had had enough and knew it was about time to wake up and tell you my story, so I put the bag down and flew home."

I rubbed my eyes. "You left it all behind?"

"Almost," Marina said. "Before I flew away, I stuck my hand in the bag and grabbed this for you."

She opened her hand, and it was the spinning top, only it had stopped moving.

"This is life," Marina said and twisted the top in her fingers. It danced across the floor. "In motion it is a thing of beauty. If you let it slow down, the chips in the wood begin to show and the fancy paint begins to fade."

I carried the top in my pocket to remind me of Marina's dream.

~~~

Marina met Ernesto when the carnival came to town. Usually fairs set up on the edge of our city with their Ferris wheels and dizzying rides. This time the trucks paraded through downtown to a big empty parking lot for a Buick dealership that closed before I was born. One tired old elephant slowly led the way while the children grabbed at his tail. Ernesto was the lion tamer, but the lion was really a bobcat with its claws pried off. Still, Ernesto walked with his head in the air, and his white shirt had not a speck of dirt on it. Of course, his blue jeans were filthy, and his big toes stuck out of his ragged shoes, but his green eyes and greasy pile of black hair kept you looking so it was hard to notice anything else.

But Marina didn't see him at all. The other girls from the high school crowded around the bobcat cage asking Ernesto questions about the sad beast. Marina, with the white hair that scared most boys her age away, was looking in the other direction. All she saw was the acrobat woman in a bathing suit covered with sequins and a hat made of
~~~

ostrich feathers. "She is the most beautiful creature," Marina said. I saw a tear sneak down Marina's cheek. To me, the woman looked no different than Mama fancied up to go out dancing, and big purple bruises were scattered on the woman's legs. But Marina stared in awe.

Marina talked Mama into going to the show that night—Papa was off somewhere playing his instrument. The three of us sat in the front row of the plastic bleachers and laughed as the clown's junky car sputtered backwards and shook ahead, burping blue smoke.

Then came the lady in the shiny swimsuit. Marina clutched Mama's shoulder and pointed as the woman climbed a tall ladder. Mama kissed Marina's cheek. "You are my girl after all," Mama said and laughed. When the woman reached the top of the ladder, she put a rope in her mouth, dropped her hands to her sides and spun in circles like my top. I could see Marina's eyes spinning around her head in time with the sparkling lady.

When Ernesto came out with the bobcat, every girl in the place had her mouth hanging open, including Mama. But not Marina. She stared at the place where the spinning lady had been. Ernesto noticed her stares and looked up, too. Seeing nothing, he shrugged and decided he must get the attention of this white–haired girl. I think Ernesto liked the challenge. He danced with his bobcat. Still Marina stared up. He dressed the beast in a baseball uniform and beat it with a plastic bat. He stuck his head sideways into the bobcat's mouth. No use. Marina stared upward as something began to spin inside of her. Mama sat up straight and smiled. I think she thought Ernesto was showing off for her, certainly not for the daughter who was so very old. Mama blinked her eyes at Ernesto and her cheeks turned a deep red.

ဗ ဗ ဗ

"The circus elephant's eyes were so beautiful and sad," Marina said. "I could tell by looking in them how very hurt he was at always having to perform for his peanuts. He seemed to be begging me, so I looked down at my chest and found a zipper. I pulled it down slowly and walked out of my skin. The elephant smiled and nodded his head. He stretched his trunk down and found his own zipper. He left an empty sack of gray in the sand. We put on each other's skins like Halloween costumes."

Marina was so alive this morning. Her hands fluttered through the air as she described the dream.

"It's not easy to be a circus elephant," she told me. "You have to watch where you step and the children tease you. But it is fun to have a trunk. I learned to fling rocks at the bearded lady. But I could not fly when I was an elephant, so I had to put my Marina skin back on and come tell you my story."

Marina and I collected empty soda bottles and turned them in at the 7–Eleven so we could buy tickets and go back to see the spinning woman each of the next three days. Mama stayed home and started moving like a madwoman, building twelve doll houses at once. It wasn't like the bill collectors were calling, but Mama would not sit still for a moment. Every day Ernesto's act got more dangerous. He would stick the bobcat with pins and then wrestle with the creature as its teeth tried to enter Ernesto's neck. He would wear the animal like a hat and spin him around until they both were dizzy. Finally, on the fourth day Marina's eyes turned to the lion tamer and she laughed at his stupid bravery. Ernesto dropped the bobcat in the dirt and walked over to kiss Marina's hand. I saw her hand begin to shake. At that moment Marina looked just like Mama to me.

Marina started crawling down the gutter drain at night when Mama was asleep or out dancing. One night I followed Marina across town and through the tall grass. I saw her meet Ernesto at the edge of the creek where Papa sometimes hunts crawdads. Marina dropped her nightgown in the rocks, and her body glowed almost as white as her hair. Ernesto stripped down to his skin, and pushed Marina into the water. I watched them splash in the water and imagined Marina trading her skin with Ernesto, just like she did with the elephant. I thought they must be in love. The carnival packed up. It was headed to San Benito next, but Ernesto stayed in our town. I think he slept in the trees and waited for Marina to come to him at night.

Marina never mentioned the spinning woman again, but I know she thought about her. Ernesto got a job in the novelty store in the mall selling fake dog vomit and black light posters of Elvis. The high school girls would crowd around the lava lamps to talk and Ernesto made sure they bought something. He was on commission. I sat on the bench outside eating a corny dog and watched it all. One day I looked through the glass and saw a woman holding Ernesto's face in both hands. He shook free, and she slapped him and ran out of the store. It was Mama.

"Marco, go home," she said. "It's not safe for you here."

Papa came home later that week to find the house littered with sections of dollhouse. Half–empty paint cans were drying into colored slush. Tiny roof shingles littered the floor. Worse yet was Mama. She walked around in her housecoat and her hair looked like a ball of yarn unwinding.

"Where the hell have you been while your family falls apart?" She screamed at Papa and ran into the bedroom.

Papa's squeezebox groaned as he dropped it to the floor. Papa rushed into the bedroom and I pressed my ear up to the closed door to hear.

"Querida, what have I done? Did someone talk about the women in the dance halls? They are my fans, I can't ignore them. I have to earn a living for my family, yes? Come kiss me and we will make up like before."

"Before your daughter wasn't the source of gossip for the town."

I imagined Mama with her hands on her hips, her eyes on fire.

"What do you say, you crazy woman?"

"I say your daughter is sneaking off with a circus boy and the neighbors are talking about the trash that lives in our house. If Marina's Grandmama were alive, she would be dying of shame. I tell you, that wicked girl will make us old before our times."

"Why are you so worried about getting old, Querida?" Papa said. "Worry only puts lines around your eyes. Be like me, let the music of life keep your feet tapping."

Mama screamed. "Old? I'll tell you old. That circus boy Ernesto tried to touch me in places you don't want to know about. That's how old I am! Our daughter is dating the devil."

Just then Marina walked in. Her cheeks were pink and she skipped into the house. "What is it, Marco?" she asked.

"It is a nightmare," I said and ran up the stairs.

∽ ∽ ∽

"I felt something icy slide along my foot and around my ankle," Marina said, and pulled the covers over us. "I decided that if I didn't move it couldn't hurt me. So I shut my eyes tight. It wove its way up my body in rings. I could feel the pointed tongue flutter on my belly. It tingled there. I held my breath knowing it would soon squeeze my chest. It whipped around my body, tighter and tighter, but I did not look. I could feel its scales pushing into my skull, stealing my thoughts.

"The pain was a dull sound that got shrill like an approaching train. I opened my eyes wide and Grandmama was over me, smiling down. She bent closer and opened her mouth over mine. Her eyes were dead and I knew then that she would drink the life from me if I let her. I reached my hand wildly in the grass growing around my bed and clutched something. It was a pink stuffed elephant from the carnival. I slapped Grandmama in the face with it and she melted like rain. Hold me, Marco."

Marina did not argue when Papa commanded her to stay away from Ernesto. I think she figured Papa would be right back on the road with his accordion and then she could do as she pleased. But Papa didn't go. His squeezebox sighed with loneliness in the corner. During the day Papa helped Mama finish the dollhouses and at night he sat on the front porch. The red glow of his cigarette guarded the door and the gun in Papa's coat was ready to deal with unwelcome visitors. I imagined Ernesto waiting in his tree for Marina, leaning his weight from one branch to another. Sometimes he dozed off, but he jerked awake before he fell. I wondered what Ernesto's dreams were like and if Marina floated into them.

Marina stopped telling me her dreams. The third day that Marina didn't come to my room, I tiptoed to hers and peeked in. Her skin and hair had became paler. "Go away, Marco," she said in a whisper dry like gravel. "I can no longer fly."

After that Marina only left her room to use the toilet. I noticed her face and body had got rounder and that she walked bent over like she was scanning the floor for the eggs of dust bunnies. She would not talk to Mama and Papa.

"I can hold out as long as you can, Marina," Mama said when she brought a tray of something that was supposed to pass for food and dropped it outside the door. Mama had traded the housecoat for a flowery dress and her hair was in pigtails. "Why must you be such a baby, Marina? We have you in our hearts."

The dollhouses were everywhere. Papa put on his Sunday suit during the week and went out to sell them to shopkeepers in all of the towns of South Texas. But even he could not keep up with Mama. She built houses like a woman possessed and she would not let anyone help her. Little girls everywhere dreamed of Mama's fancy houses and their parents struggled to pay the price. Money poured into our home like green honey, but Mama did not stop. Marina stayed in her bed and dreamed secret dreams.

Mama and Papa stopped talking to each other in sentences of more than five words.

"The houses sold well today," Papa would say.

"Buy more wood and paint," Mama would reply.

Papa did not sleep. His face turned gray and drooped from the nights spent guarding the porch. No one had seen Ernesto. He no longer showed up for work at the novelty store and sales were said to be off. I imagined him out in the woods watching the red dot of the cigarette as it traveled up to Papa's mouth and down again like a cherry on fire.

Then one night Papa's eyelids became too heavy and he fell into a deep, dreamy sleep. I awoke upstairs to the sound of an owl outside my window. His bird questions were loud and demanding, but I had no answers. Then there was a crash downstairs and a gunshot.

I ran to the staircase and saw Papa swinging the pistol in the air. "Get back in bed, Marco," he yelled up at me. "I will protect my house."

I raced to my room and stuck my nose against the cold window. I saw Ernesto running from Papa and the gun. Ernesto was carrying something. He swung it around and knocked Papa to the ground. The last I saw of Ernesto he was disappearing into the night cradling Papa's squeezebox.

In the morning I heard Papa load the rest of the completed doll houses into his truck—except one Mama left in front of Marina's door to cheer her up—so they could be sold in town. I looked out the window and did not recognize him. The suit was baggy and he walked as if under gray water. He honked once for Mama and they drove away. I knew they would not return for hours.

I thought I heard the owl again, but knew it could not be so in daylight. The sound was faint, like a mouse crying in the wall. I opened my bedroom door and realized the sound was coming from Marina's room. I opened the door and saw Marina's bed had become huge. She seemed but a tiny dot in a huge sea of sheets.

"Marco, I have a dream," she said.

"Not now, Marina. You are sick. Let me get a doctor."

Her tiny chest forced its way up and down and her cloudy white hair was damp. "Listen first, Marco. Please."

"Okay," I said and sat on the edge of the bed.

"In the dream I am asleep in my bed, but our house has no roof. The sun shines down on me, warming my soul." Marina's eyes smiled at me. "I got up and stretched my arms twenty feet over my head. It felt so good to move about. I walked downstairs and out the front door. Mama was painting the house a bright pink. 'Whatever you do, you mustn't drink from the river,' she told me.

"I looked out across the river and saw Grandmama on the other side in a rocking chair doing her knitting. She smiled and said, 'I told you I'd see you soon, Marina. When I'm done with those baby booties we will have us a long talk.' I could hear her words, but she must have been five miles away. She looked back down at her knitting, then she seemed to remember something. She looked up and said, 'You're too old to be drinking from that river, Marina.'"

Marina's voice was becoming softer and softer. She pulled me close to whisper the rest of her dream.

"The sun was beating down on me and I was dripping sweat from the heat. But it felt so very good. I stripped off my clothes and sat in the grass watching Mama paint and Grandmama rock. The more I watched them the drier my throat became. My teeth were turning to sand and my tongue swelled like the elephant's trunk. I was so very thirsty.

"I waited until Mama was concentrating on painting the shutters and dashed across the field. 'Stop that this instant, Marina! Act like an adult,' Mama yelled behind me. I reached the river's edge and kneeled at the bank. Grandmama shook her head and said, 'Save some for me, dear.' I dunked my head in the water and breathed it. I could feel it flow out my fingers and toes. I began to float. I rose up over the river. Mama and Grandmama waved from below. They became tiny specks as I went higher and higher into the sky."

Marina's eyes began to flutter. "Marina, I'm scared," I said.

Her eyes cleared and she smiled at me. "Marco, I just returned to say goodbye. Grandmama says to be a good boy," she said, and closed her eyes.

I did not know what to do. I almost tripped over the dollhouse in the doorway as I ran downstairs to look for something, anything. Medicine, heavy weights to put on her feet and pull her back. All I found were dollhouse parts. I grabbed an open can of black paint and brought it to Marina. I poured it on her hair and worked it in. My hands began to turn to night. Somewhere behind my eyes I could see Marina getting smaller and younger by the second. She was flying again. Then Grandmama's wrinkled, gray hands came down from nowhere and plucked the dollhouse up into the sky like it was a cloud. I saw tiny baby Marina float into the little pink doorway. She was laughing when Grandmama shut the door tight. ☙

THE SCREENWRITER

WHEN HE SEES ME carrying the greasy bag, Marco grabs a burger and bites into it immediately.

"You weren't kidding!" He gnaws off another bite before lifting his greasy mouth. "Where did you get these?"

"I'll keep the location of the best cheeseburger in town a secret to my own grave."

He swallows another bite and looks up.

"Get these to Charlie Wright, stat."

"You heard that on a television show," I say.

"And I've always wanted to say it."

"How's he doing?" Marco sets the burger on the counter.

"Better. The dying often have a surge before passing on. It's when they say their last goodbyes. This may be it. Don't be late."

"Think he'll be able to eat this?"

"If he doesn't, I will."

ꕥ ꕥ ꕥ

I stick my hand through the partially open door and shake the bag.

"Get the hell in here!" Mr. Wright says.

The Christmas tree is set up in the corner with presents and crackly pine needles crowding its bottom. Carla and Bob are casually slumped in chairs on either side of a table on top of which rests a pink frosted cake and Mr. Wright's artificial leg, which has been decorated with a Santa hat and a lipstick face.

"You know the chorus of John Jacob Jingleheimer Schmidt?" Carla says. "We were singing."

"Badly," Mr. Wright says.

"Dad keeps talking about a man in white who visits him," she says.

"He's in the corner laughing right now," Mr. Wright says.

"I told him it's Elvis," Bob says.

Mr. Wright's eyelids are droopy, and he drifts away for a moment. When his eyes open, he reaches out a hand.

"Gimme."

I peel back the paper on a burger and place it in his hand. He takes a big bite and gives me a thumbs up.

"That's more like it! Red meat to fuel the blast off."

"We've been telling stories, too," Carla says. 'Like the first time Mike smoked a joint in front of Dad. He was sixteen and had hair down to his shoulders."

"My boy the hippie pothead," Mr. Wright says.

He takes one more bite then lets the burger rest on the sheet.

"Mike was a rebel." Mr. Wright stares toward the window and I wonder if his son is sitting there. "He never knew how much that crap stank."

"It helps to have a big brother," Bob says. "They break in the parents for us youngsters."

"And they provide impossible role models," Carla says.

"She thinks her husband looks like Mike," Bob says.

"Where is your husband?" I ask.

"Business trip," she says.

"He takes after the old man," Mr. Wright says.

He lifts his burger high in the air.

"Here's to Mike and the husband. We'll forgive them, if they'll forgive us!"

"Here, here," Carla says.

"There, there," Bob says.

I look around at their grins and realize they mean it. The great gift Mr. Wright has given his children is acceptance and forgiveness, and I do believe they've returned it to him. I think of my own father's quick passing and can't be more jealous.

ೞ ೞ ೞ

We eat cake, sip at whiskey, and tell stories until almost midnight. Somewhere along the way the kids open presents for their father. Mr. Wright slips in and out of consciousness. When he's awake, he picks at his pajamas like they're covered with bugs.

Carla motions for me to go into the hallway.

"We need to do the rest of this by ourselves," she says when we're alone. "As a family. No offense."

I feel my face redden. I'd almost forgotten my only true role here is as scribe of death.

"Gotcha," I say. "But I'm going to lurk. I have to know when it's over. I can't find out in the newspaper obituary. Just give me five minutes or so to say goodbye."

"Sure. Bob and I could use a break. It's getting harder to keep the smile from cracking."

"You're lucky."

She laughs and reaches out to hold me. Her hair smells of sweet corn.

"I sure don't feel like it, but thanks. For everything."

ᔓ ᔓ ᔓ

I pull a chair close to Mr. Wright's bed.

"Charlie," I whisper.

His eyelids flutter open. The skin on his face is becoming translucent.

"You've never told me about your acting," I say. "I'm guessing community theater?"

His face gets mock serious, and he puckers his lips.

"All the world's a stage, my boy, and I shall depart in the third act."

"I think we're there," I say.

"Verily. And I'm okay with it. The great mystery awaits."

He reaches over and takes my hand.

"How are my kids really taking this?"

"Pretty well. Better than I did. But that was different."

"Tell me about it, Matt. I need to know." ᔓ

MATT

I AWOKE INTO A new year with the worst hangover of my life. My head throbbed and I realized I'd been asleep for four hours, tops. My roommate Pete was shaking me, saying something about the telephone. My eyelids were half stuck together and my mouth, you didn't want to know about my mouth. Pete and our other roommate, Steve—we were all radio–television–film majors and wannabe directors—had come back to campus early so we could host the biggest New Year's Eve party known to man, or at least to our college. While those two were at home opening Christmas presents and stuffing their faces with turkey, I had stayed in our broken–down rent house, swaddled in blankets, avoiding my family.

I went downstairs and picked up the phone. It was my sister Sara calling from Houston. She said Dad was in the hospital and it didn't look good. He had called her and complained of chest pains late last night. She sounded bad. Sara'd been there all night and she'd had even less sleep than I'd had.

My Dad. Except for his regular monthly rent check deliveries at the McDonald's out on the interstate, I hadn't *really* talked to him since last semester. Not since he'd shown up at our house drunk and started crying and talking about Mom, saying it was all his fault she'd walked out on us. No argument there.

Sara was a paramedic and she started giving me the medical run down. Blood pressure and all that. Dad was in intensive care with machines helping him to breathe, she said. What it came down to was I'd better get to Houston fast. There was a half–full cup of warm beer left over from last night's party balanced on the railing. I chugged it down in one gulp. It tasted of cigarette butts.

I stripped out of my underwear, climbed in the shower, and stood under the cold water for a while hoping the shock would clear my head. The thing was, I'd always been able to tell when the ones I cared about were going to die. I remembered I'd been about six years old when my mother had come to my door. She hadn't had to say a thing. I knew. I said, "It's Ransom, isn't it?" Ransom was my dog—I fed him and cleaned up after him. He'd died that morning. Just curled up on this old blanket he liked to chew on and died. He left a little turd by his butt and a puddle next to that. I'd kept expecting my Mom to get mad and tell me to clean it up like she usually did when Ransom would make a mess in the house. This time she didn't say a word, except to tell my Dad to dig a grave in the backyard. After that, I always imagined dying as letting the plug out of a bathtub. Everything slowly draining away.

Sara said Dad had been in good spirits and joking around on the way to the hospital. After they arrived was when it got serious. The doctor said the strain on his body from the heart attack might have brought on the stroke.

I was thinking this was a dream. Like in the movies. Maybe if I went back to sleep. I curled up at the bottom of the shower with my head between my legs and let the water cover me. My Dad was the only guy I ever met who was both skinny and flabby at the same time. He was tall and reed thin, but his shoulders bent forward toward a bulging stomach. He'd always been a mass of contradictions. One minute he pushed me to succeed, the next he made me feel like a complete failure. I remembered when I was in junior high he'd refused to help me with my math homework. Math came easily to him and he kept telling me I was stupid.

"You've got to learn to stand up and do things on your own, Matt," he said.

I was frustrated as hell. I put my head down on my book and started crying. That really pissed him off.

"You're not even trying!" he'd yelled and stomped out of my bedroom.

Another time he'd tried to teach me to dive. The whole family went to the lake for the 4th of July. I think I was six. Dad started by having me kneel at the edge of the dock and lean forward into the water. Sara swam in the water in front of me shouting words of encouragement and hanging on to this huge inflatable life preserver that was shaped like a pencil, with an eraser even. I fell in the water stomach first, sending shock waves of water toward Sara.

"No! No, Matt!" Dad said. "What's the point of this if you're not going to do it right?"

He'd stood on the dock like a lifeguard with his arms crossed at his chest, one foot resting on an ice chest. I climbed the rope ladder and knelt in front of him again. I concentrated with all my might, leaning slowly, my hands cupped together as if I were praying. I fell. The water drenched my face a split second before my stomach.

"You're getting it!" Mom yelled and giggled loudly from the shore. "That's enough for now, don't you think, Gene?" she said to Dad.

He shook his head and stomped his foot down on the dock.

"He can do better. Perfection, that's the only real goal."

I was at the top of the ladder. He'd looked down on me and his face had softened. He extended a hand to me.

"It's okay, Matt. I couldn't do anything when I was your age either."

At that moment, I'd wanted to take Sara's huge pencil and erase my Dad completely.

ꕥ ꕥ ꕥ

Pete pulled me up from the shower floor.

"Snap out of it," he said.

I told him I needed to borrow his car. Pete had been giving me shit just last week about borrowing his machine all the time. My Dad had offered to buy me a car, but I kept turning him down. I liked to ride my bicycle instead. It seemed to get me where I wanted to go faster.

Pete said, "No problem," and handed me his car keys. He didn't even ask me why. I didn't know if he was feeling guilty or if the look on my face scared him.

Once I got on the highway, I realized I was crying. I could feel the heat as the tears rolled down my face, but they felt alien, like a special effect from one of my film classes. I wondered if all these hung–over drivers were secretly cringing because they had to give up New Year's Day to sit with their families, watch boring football games on TV, and eat way too much food. I could hear my dad now: "Sacrifice is the key to success." But the only place he was a success was in the business world. Mostly he was a lonely drunk. I'd noticed when I saw him last semester that his face had gotten all bloated and gray. He was old. He'd stopped being Mr. Invincible for me years ago, but he was never an old man. He'd come by the house and picked me up. It was strange to see Dad in the doorway of Bedford Falls. Pete was a huge fan of Frank Capra films and came up with that name for our rent house, which was ironic given the amount of drunken debauchery that went on there. Dad drove me around town and swilled on this flask full of gin. I finally took him to a club where the locals hung out, figuring nobody I knew from school would spot us there. It was called the Wheeler Dealer Club. Seriously. Dad pinched the waitress on the ass, and she actually didn't seem to mind. But then he'd started saying how Mom was the only woman he'd ever really loved and how she finally couldn't put up with him any more and "hopped on the bus, Gus." He'd actually said that.

I'd had about all I could take and maybe a few too many beers from the Wheeler Dealer trough. I was thinking what I'd really like to tell the old man. Something like: "You're right. She had all she could stand of you and I don't blame her. You're shrinking. You know that? I think you're about five inches shorter than you were three years ago. A few more years and you'll be gone."

I sipped my beer and kept quiet.

Dad had told me not to blame myself for Mom leaving. He'd said she'd left because of him; Sara and I hadn't had a thing to do with it. Maybe that was why I hadn't seen my mother since I was in high school. One day in my senior year, she'd left a roll of quarters on the kitchen table for my lunch money, and vanished.

Dad fell asleep at the Wheeler Dealer. I'd had to check his pockets for a motel key and drive him back. I tucked him in, like he did me when I was a little kid. He used to put me to sleep by reading *The Little Engine That Could*. I could still remember his throaty voice repeating, "I think I can, I think I can ..."

ᔕ ᔕ ᔕ

I pulled into the parking garage at Methodist Hospital. A machine buzzed and spit a red ticket at me. I was pretty much in one piece when I walked in, except I couldn't breathe right. I figured maybe it was that too–clean hospital smell. I asked for my Dad, and this dark–skinned nurse with big eyes scanned a chart and got grimly businesslike. She said, "Follow the yellow line to intensive care."

The tears started again when I saw Sara sitting there pretending to read a magazine. She was only two years older than me, but she looked ancient without makeup and dressed in that hurry–up, nothing–matches way. She saw me and reached out. We were not really a hugging family, but, I thought, maybe it wasn't too late to start and wrapped my arms around her.

"It's all right, Matt," she said, pushing the hair out of my eyes. "He isn't conscious right now, but we can see him in a few minutes. Don't be shocked. He doesn't look the same."

We had to wait in this room with really uncomfortable chairs. I guessed they figured if you were waiting in here you couldn't relax. I somehow dozed off for a little while anyway, until Sara woke me and said we could go in.

It was like a stable with all these stalls, only instead of horses they were full of old people hooked up to machines that were blinking and making noises. My Dad didn't look good. In fact, he didn't look much like my father. I couldn't begin to guess what all the machinery was doing, except forcing him to breathe in a mechanical wheeze. His bloated stomach lifted and fell, lifted and fell. There were tubes everywhere—in his arms, in his nose.

"Nice outfit, Dad," I said. His eyes rolled back in their sockets, but he didn't notice me. Silver stubble shone from his pale face. God, he looked old.

My chest felt tight when Sara showed me back to the waiting room. The crowd cleared after visiting time. Sara said they'd all be back in another two hours like clockwork.

"Get some sleep," I told her. "You can't do anything else."

She frowned and crossed her hands at her chest in resistance, but finally said, "Okay."

A lanky guy in a worn cowboy hat gave her a pillow and she stretched out on the couch. This guy and his family stayed around when everybody else left. At least I assumed it was his family. There were three guys in their thirties or forties talking about business stuff and two women who were either their sisters or wives. One really old lady was reading a Reader's Digest and leaning in close to a lamp.

"What you in for?" the guy in the cowboy hat asked me. He looked like the sheriff in an old John Wayne flick.

"It's my father," I said.

He nodded.

"Mine, too. I'm Otis."

Otis had flown in from Amarillo that morning with his wife, the bleached blonde crocheting over by the phone and arguing with Otis' sister about whether Nikki and Lyle, two characters on a soap opera, would ever get married.

I tried to sleep, but I heard one of Otis' brothers-in-law talking about how good their old man had looked during the last visiting hour.

"Say, how much property does he have anyway?" he said.

I lifted my eyelids and saw him scratch at the spot where his stomach hung loose from his shirt. Otis propped his boots on the coffee table and looked hard at his relative.

The waiting room phone rang and a nurse said it was for Sara. Sara's eyes got wide after she picked up the receiver. She talked for a while and smiled over at me and laughed. I figured she was filling in some long lost relative on the details of Dad's illness. Sara was her normal self—in total control. Ever since I'd been in diapers, I'd thought of her as the one who kept our house from falling apart. Our parents had made Sara and me take baths together every other night, but it felt more like Sara giving me a bath. She'd soaped up my hair and pulled it out into long tufts on the sides.

"Why, it's Bozo the clown!" she screamed.

We laughed until Dad came in and told us to shut up.

"You're disturbing your mother," he said and grabbed us by the hair on top of our heads.

He lifted us up out of the bathtub and dangled our shivering bodies in the cold air. According to Dad, everything Sara and I had done as kids annoyed our mother. He liked to call us his Little Monkeys.

I'd been right about the phone caller—it was a long–lost relative.

"Matt, don't get upset, but that was Mom," Sara said. "She's coming in a couple of hours. I told her you'd pick her up at the airport."

"How'd she–" I started to say. My head throbbed again and I could smell last night's alcohol seeping out of my skin.

"I phoned Grandma Simms, and she called her for me. The old bitch still wouldn't give me Mom's number. Anyway, Mom's coming. She'll be here at one, and I told her you'd meet her."

Sara had never liked my mother's mother, an aging debutante who wouldn't forgive Mom for marrying beneath her. Grandma Simms didn't care much for the offspring the marriage produced either, and had steadfastly refused to divulge Mom's whereabouts for the last three years.

Sara started giggling.

"I'm glad you think this is funny," I said and wiped a fine line of sweat off my upper lip.

"No, it's not that," she said and shook her head. "I was just remembering that time Mom rescued you from Terri Titzel and her mother."

"Oh, yeah, Tits," I said.

Sara and I both raised our hands to our mouths to stifle giggles.

Terri Titzel had been the first girl in our elementary school to grow breasts, and her family's name hadn't helped make matters easier for her with sexually obsessed sixth–grade boys, including me.

"That was when your story–telling problem got really bad," Sara said.

As a kid I'd told everybody that I went to Mars at night. My green alien friends would land their saucers on the roof and zip me away for a fun–filled evening. Then I'd seen the movie *Harvey* and developed my own imaginary friend. I called him Clarence and blamed him for everything. By the time I hit puberty, my parents were used to my tales of Clarence breaking lamps and leaving the empty water jug in the refrigerator. By the time of the incident with Terri Titzel, I was obsessed with whatever movie I'd seen last on television. If it was a western, I'd go around shooting everyone; if it was a horror film, I became Dracula and wanted to suck blood. Then I saw *The Graduate.*

"I can't believe you asked Tits if her mother wanted to seduce you," Sara said and laughed through her fingers.

One of Otis the cowboy's relatives—a sister, I think—frowned at us.

Terri had told Mrs. Titzel what I'd said and called my mother immediately, screaming about "that boy, the pervert." Mom had stood up for me and refused to believe I would say any such thing. I could still see her with her hands at her hips leaning into Mrs. Titzel's face, yelling, "My son has better taste than that, you fat sow!"

Sara, Dad, and I had hovered around Mom in the kitchen that night as she prepared dinner. We'd wondered who this woman was.

"Don't forget who believed in you, Matt," Dad had said, his eyes wet with adoration for Mom. Then he'd looked away. I'd been sure he'd seen right through me.

ᔕ ᔕ ᔕ

There wasn't much change during the next bi–hourly cattle call. It was time to go to the airport and get my mother.

The plane was late, of course. I didn't even know where she was coming from. Her flight was from Dallas, but they all came from Dallas. Once again I was sitting in a waiting room. I rested my feet on a metal ashtray and settled in. There was something weirdly exciting about airports—all of that arriving and leaving. Every time I'd had to meet someone's plane, I'd secretly imagined Mom walking out of the little tunnel twirling her hair around a finger and saying, "Hi, honey. I'm back. It'll all be better now."

God, here we were.

If this were a comic film—the kind I hoped to make someday—I'd be pacing back and forth, maybe knocking stuff over, in anticipation. Instead I sat waiting for that tingle in my stomach like on a roller coaster when you start to fall straight down. But all I could feel was last night's stale beer sloshing around inside me. I was staring down the tunnel and trying not to puke, when a hand tapped me on the shoulder.

"Mom?" She didn't look like the one I remembered. She must have walked right past me. Her gray hair was cropped close to her ears. Mine was probably longer.

"I look a little different, don't I?" she said in a nasal way I didn't remember. She had a big smile. I couldn't help cynically imagining her practicing it on the airplane. That perfect combination of concern and cheerfulness, maybe a little fear around the edges. She was wearing a jogging suit, a red one with white stripes down the sides of her legs. Her skin was tan, her body athletically trim. She looked like those women who drink diet shakes religiously, not the lumpily soft woman I remembered giving me a tiny metal four–leaf clover for luck when I played my first Little League game. We'd lost, and I had given the good–luck charm back a week later after Mom yelled at me for coming home an hour late. Dad wouldn't let her give me the charm again, ever. On principle, he said.

"Sara will be glad to see you," I told Mom. I couldn't think of anything else to say to this familiar stranger.

"How is Sara?" She asked as we headed past the gift shop—*Welcome to Houston. It's Not the Heat, It's the Stupidity,* the T–shirts read, even during winter.

"Oh, she's a rock, Mom, a rock." I said. "I'm the one who's a mess. But you know that."

She got quiet.

"Matt, please, let's not do this now. I'm here for your father."

"Oh, I'm sure he'll be glad to see you, too," I said as we walked into the parking lot.

I opened the door to Pete's car a little too sharply.

"Maybe I deserve that," Mom said. "Do you have to attack now? I should have said I'm here for you and Sara. Can we call a truce for now?"

"Okay," I said.

I didn't have the strength to fight anyway. The last thing I'd eaten was bean dip and I'd washed that down with enough keg beer to fill a good–sized kiddy pool. We considered stopping for burgers, but Mom said she was worried about Sara.

Instead we stopped in the hospital cafeteria on the way in and bought a pile of junk food. Potato chips, Cokes, Zingers, cheese crackers. When I didn't eat for a while I got the shakes. Right then my muscles felt like steel. I grabbed some yogurt for Sara. Vanilla. She was always on a diet.

It was visiting time when we got upstairs, and the waiting room was crowded with worried families. Otis the cowboy nodded from the corner. Sara grabbed Mom and they headed through the double doors to see the old man. I picked up a six–month–old magazine and pretended to read. "How to Take Years Off Your Figure," it said on the cover.

I was dozing in a pile of assorted crumbs when this bald doctor walked in. He steered Otis the cowboy's family over to the corner. I guess it was like on TV where you moved over a few feet and suddenly nobody could hear a thing you said.

"To be honest, folks, we've been very worried about him," the doctor said, laying out everything he learned in Bedside Manner 101. "In most cases he wouldn't still be here with us. But we're not talking most cases."

Otis nibbled on his fingertips.

"What's the story, Doc?"

"Please, I'm sorry if I've scared you," the doctor said, with this big grin that seems to say the opposite. "We don't see this one too often. It's common in pigs, but rather uncommon with people. Your father did his own natural heart bypass. When the artery closed up, he switched over to a new one. He's a lucky man."

"He's going to be okay?" the old lady asked. This had to be Otis's mom. She adjusted her flowered hat and leaned forward.

"I can't guarantee anything, but, yes, I think he'll be fine. He'll need to change his diet and start getting more exercise, of course, but he'll be fine."

"Now, he shouldn't be roaming around a lot, like on a ranch or anything, should he, doctor?" asked the brother-in-law with the sizable gut and pants starting halfway down the crack of his ass. He had a concerned yet hungry look.

"Actually, the exercise would probably do him good if it's not too strenuous," the doc said.

"Now, do you hear that, Mother Covert?" The gut man winked at Otis. "Now, I know we'd all be happy to help out with the place. At least till he gets back on his feet."

Otis started to get red around the neck.

"I think Daddy can make those kind of decisions when he gets home, Elmer. Unless you'd like to go in there and bring it up with him now."

That seemed to settle things.

Mom and Sara came out—no change, but the doctor wanted to talk to us soon. We munched on the rest of the junk food and mostly kept quiet. Mom found the stairwell where the orderlies smoked their cigarettes and slipped out from time to time. Despite her healthy appearance, she still smoked a lot. Sara talked to the nurses. She spoke their language and kept us up to date.

I must have heard that damn pig story thirty times in the next hour. "I always knew he was a pig, but this is ridiculous." Yuck, yuck. "All those years of makin' bacon paid off." Wink, wink. Despite the good news, most of Otis's family decided to stick around. It may have been my paranoia, but I could feel them staring. I guess we beat watching soap operas back in the motel.

The doctor looked like a young Alan Alda from the early *M*A*S*H* episodes. He had dark half moons under his eyes, and this time there was no mistaking whose turn it was. Every member of Otis's family suddenly discovered really great stories in their magazines, but I still felt their beady eyes boring in.

Dad was getting worse, was the gist of what the doctor told us. They could operate, but his organs were in such bad shape from all the years of boozing, it probably would kill him. They kept pumping medicine in him, but it wasn't doing the trick. If they didn't do anything, he'd probably die.

"There's not much we can do but wait," the doctor said, staring me in the eyes. "The decision you have is whether to make an all–out effort—remember, it probably would do more harm than good—or let him go. The final choice is yours, but frankly I advise you to let him go peacefully. I'm sorry."

Sara looked at me and started shaking. Tears started rolling down her cheeks for the first time since I'd shown up. Mom looked like a deer caught in a Cadillac's headlights. Shit. The doctor was looking at me. I finally figured out he expected me to tell him what to do. I realized I was crying again, full force. I couldn't turn it off.

"Sara?" Her head was buried in Mom's lap. "Yeah. Let him go," I said.

I got up. I absolutely could not breathe. A pair of eyes topped an old *Newsweek*. "Spy Sells Secret Defense Plans," the headline read. I grabbed the magazine out of her hands and stared into Otis's mom's faded blue eyes.

"My Dad hated pork," I said, dropped the magazine to the floor and walked out.

I could hear her whispering behind me. She must've thought I was crazy.

I pushed open a door and this black guy in white was smoking a cigarette. I bummed one, a Kool, and sat down on the concrete steps. My Dad used to be a rock. There had been a time when he was the final word on anything. My oldest memory of him—at least I believed it was a memory, my mother might have told it to me—was when I was about three. I had the hose running in the backyard and I'd lined up my little green plastic soldiers for muddy battle. Suddenly my legs had felt like they were on fire. I screamed and scraped at them with my fingernails. Dad appeared out of nowhere, grabbed me, and stripped my pants off, then my shirt. I'd been covered with ants almost up to my waist.

"Don't worry, Matt. I'll protect you. There wasn't an ant born that could beat your old Dad."

He'd hoisted me onto his shoulders and carried me inside at a trot. He put me on his lap and turned the TV to cartoons to calm me down. It had worked. I remembered his gentle hands as he rubbed lotion onto my bites. My tears had been almost dry when he'd said in the voice of experience, "It's time you became a big boy, Matt. You get strong and be a man, and nothing can ever hurt you again."

He'd thought he was doing me a favor with those words of wisdom, giving me the benefit of his years of experience, but the truth was I'd had no desire whatsoever to be a "big boy." I'd just wanted to play. It had been his job to be grown up.

Mom came out and squatted on the step beneath me. She pulled a pack of Virginia Slims out of her purse and lit one up. Sandi, Pete's girlfriend, smoked the same brand, but she called them Vagina Slimes. Sandi was always looking to shock somebody with her high school bathroom humor. Last night, Sandi and I had talked for hours. I'd actually cried on her shoulder about spending my Christmas alone at school, and joked that I watched *It's a Wonderful Life* over and over again and ate turkey hotdogs.

"My family died in a car wreck when I was in high school," I'd told her, not veering too far from the truth, if you asked me.

"Don't lie, asshole," she'd said and flicked a tear off my nose. "Maybe you should quit hiding in this house." She'd kissed me on the cheek. "It's just a suggestion."

I dropped the cigarette stump and ground it out with my tennis shoe. Mom handed me a Slime to replace it.

"I was 33 when my father died. I didn't find out till I was 35," Mom offered. She was trying. I couldn't blame her for that. "He left when I was still a little girl. Your grandmother's devotion to the church probably drove him out. He told me that he had a hole in his soul, and life wouldn't be quite right until he found something to fill it. I asked him, with my best little girl logic, why didn't he go down to the shoe repair place and have them fix it. He roared at that one, but he said this hole couldn't be filled at any one place. He said he had to move around a little to get it all. I missed him terribly."

I remembered seeing pictures of him. Skinny with a million wrinkles. "He was a bum, Mom."

"No, Matt, he was a hobo," she said, narrowing her eyes for a second. "There's a difference. My father always said bums were lazy and—worse—bored. Hobos worked for a living, he'd said. They had to keep moving around to fill that hole up. His eyes had lit up when he talked about traveling. Actually, I think there's a lot of your grandfather in you, Matt."

"Yeah? I don't notice me doing any leaving," I said, pulling my knees up to my chin. "In fact, I think I'm one of the few people around here who can claim that."

I regretted the words before they were all the way out of my mouth.

Mom took a deep drag off her cigarette and stared down the staircase. I cupped my cigarette inside my hand when a couple of doctors pushed past and gave us that cigarettes–are–going–to–kill–you stare. The doctors pointed sternly toward the exit. Mom giggled as we went out into the cool afternoon air. We wandered onto the lawn and sat on a bench near the edge of the hospital grounds. I looked down the street from us and saw a shirtless man pushing a small boy on a bicycle. He was trying to teach the boy to ride, but he didn't want to let go of the kid's bike. The boy and bicycle wobbled in his hands. I remembered my Dad had promised to teach me to ride, too, but it was Sara who'd finally done it. I'd been seven and all my friends had been riding bikes for at least a year. I'd been desperate to join them. I'd sat atop the pink banana seat of her bike and she'd pushed me down the street until I forgot she was there. When I'd looked back, she was half a block behind me. I freaked out and tried to put my bare feet down to stop. Instead, I'd rammed her bicycle into the side of Mom's car. My feet had looked like hamburger and a deep scratch ran along the driver's side of the car. Sara'd pulled me off the pavement and said, with a gleam in her eye, "So, you mean you wanted to learn how to stop, too?" Sara had been grounded for the dent in the car; I'd gotten my own bicycle and I'd been pedaling ever since.

Mom leaned across the bench and put her hand on my sleeve. "Where'd you learn to do that trick with the cigarette?" she asked. You pointed the cigarette into your hand with the tip of the filter barely between your fingers. The smoke and the smell gave you away, but it hid the butt for a couple of seconds.

I told her that was how we'd hid it from her back in junior high, back before. Then I went for broke and looked her in the eyes.

"Why did you do it? I mean, the old man isn't all that much, but you did marry him. And Sara and I weren't angels, but we weren't that bad, were we? Or did your father teach you it's better to disappear?"

Her mouth tightened.

"I loved your father. I still love your father," she said. "Maybe you're right, maybe I am my daddy's girl."

She laughed and tilted her head back. For a second, she looked a lot like Sara.

"It wasn't planned. I never meant to hurt anybody. I was going to call you kids, but I wanted to get settled first and I kept putting it off."

"Oh, that's a hell of an excuse. I can see the review now: 'Mother procrastinates: Can't remember where she put those pesky kids. Two and a Half Stars.'"

"Dammit, Matt," she said. "After a while I figured I didn't have the right to interfere with your lives. Maybe I was afraid of this. Of having to deal with the guilt. It may be hard for you to believe, but I thought about you and Sara all the time."

She put her cheek to my knee and opened the floodgates. I stroked her hair and pretty soon I was crying, too. It was becoming a habit. I should have cried myself dry by now. After a while, Mom told me how she'd stayed with a cousin of hers up in New York until she'd landed a job typesetting for a little newspaper. Turned out she now had her own printing business with five employees. I guess in a way she was still handing out the lunch money.

Finally we went back in and found Sara ordering nurses around and apparently truly pissing them off near the intensive care waiting room. Some old college buddy of Dad's had shown up out of nowhere and tried to regale us with stories about the panty raids he and the old man pulled in the dinosaur days.

I grabbed Sara and tried to sit her down, but she gave me a look that left second degree burns.

"Fuck off, Matt."

She jerked her arm free and went back through the double doors to intensive care.

I was amazed when I looked at the clock and it was almost 5 p.m. When had I lost the concept of time? There was not much left for us to do but sit around and wait, anyway.

I dozed off and had a dream I'd been having a lot lately. I was late for class, but I couldn't remember the room number. I finally found it, but the professor came over and asked who I was, like I was from Mars or something. Seemed I hadn't made it to class in a few months. Then I realized the professor was my father. "I think you can, Little Monkey," he said in a monotone. Dad stared at me and his eyes were completely black. I gazed into them and the blackness sank into my skin. I felt it flowing in my veins. I looked at my hands and they began to disappear. A nurse shook me awake. "They want you in there, sir. It's time."

Sara and Mom were standing over the bed when I came in. Sara put her arms around me and sobbed into my shirt, her mouth wide. Mom gave me that look that said, yep, this was the real thing.

"We're all here with you, Gene," Mom said to Dad. "Me and Sara and Matt."

The old man's eyelids blinked, but his eyeballs were still roaming around freely in his head. His left cheek tightened slightly. I walked with Sara to the bed and grabbed his hand. It was like ice. Rough ice.

"I hear you've been stealing women's panties, Dad," I told him. Why had I said that? What the hell was going on?

I felt I should say something else, but I couldn't. I was thinking: "Your Little Monkey loves you, old man. You picked a hell of a time to run. You'd never told me it would be like this, Dad." But I couldn't say it. I just leaned over, gripping his fingers tighter. He smelled of Old Spice and dusty urine.

Sara tried to pull me back from the bed, but I could swear the old man was pulling, too. Pulling me in. I let go and his fist flew to his chest. One of the big machines emitted a low hum. A straight line ran across it. Just like on television.

A young priest appeared out of nowhere, grabbed our hands, and started praying. "Our Father, who art in heaven. Hallowed be thy name…" It was like a stale script: Priest enters, stage left. Family grieves.

I wriggled my hand free from the priest's and he looked at me helplessly. Mom held Sara tight. Sara held Mom even tighter. None of us were chanting on cue.

"He was Catholic, wasn't he?" the priest asked, shrugging his shoulders.

"Yeah," I said, wiping my shirtsleeve across my face. "I think my grandparents were at least."

A nurse herded us into this little room off from the waiting room. The Bereaved Room, I guessed. No telling how many people had been there before us. McDeath. Over a billion served. Some administrator wanted us to sign forms. She wanted to know where the body should go. Sign here and here.

"Can you give us a fucking minute?" Sara screamed. Her eyes were like fire. "My father just died!"

I guess you couldn't bury him in the backyard, I thought. I started to wonder how these people played this same scene out over and over.

"I'll take care of it, Sara," Mom said and grabbed her arm. "Then let's all go home."

I was thinking: I'd be happy to if someone would be so kind as to tell me where the hell home was. But I kept my mouth shut and walked Sara down the stairs and out the door into the cool air. The sun was beginning to set. We went back to the same bench Mom and I had sat on earlier.

"Happy holidays, Matt," Sara said with a weak grin.

She closed her eyes tightly and pressed her face to my chest. We sat there like that for a long time, and I could feel an icy breeze sting my hair.

I looked out at the street and saw the father and son bicyclists at it again—or maybe they'd never stopped. This time the boy was riding a little more steadily. Two slightly older kids were ahead of them, waiting impatiently on their own bikes, popping wheelies and riding in circles. The man ran beside the bicycle and held the boy up by the armpits. They went about ten feet like that, and then the man suddenly let go.

The kid's face tightened and he pedaled furiously for a few feet. The bicycle listed toward the curb. Just before it crashed, the man grabbed the kid and jerked the bicycle upright. Then they did it all over again. And again. And again.

I watched until they turned the corner and disappeared from view, the older boys leading the way. At that moment there were only two things in life about which I was certain. One, eventually the man would have to let that bicycle crash, and, two, the boy would spend the rest of his life learning how to forgive him. ಲ

THE SCREENWRITER

"FORGIVE HIM," MR. WRIGHT says.

"Yeah, I need to."

"I mean it." His words are soft and slow. "Forgiveness is more important than being right. If I'm to die with any belief that my own kids can forgive me, I need to know you can do it, too."

I look toward the window.

"Do you see him?"

"I think so," Mr. Wright says. "He's waving at you."

"Don't bullshit me."

Mr. Wright smiles.

"I can't tell you what it's like to die. I only know what it's like to be in this bed and wonder if I'm about to pass over to something, anything."

"I'm afraid for you," I say.

"Fear is the devil, son."

"Then I guess he's got me."

"I know your Dad is listening, Matt. Love never ends. And if he's not listening, I am."

Words quiver from my throat, and tears drip down my face.

"I forgive you, Dad."

"Good boy."

Mr. Wright raises his hand and sketches the sign of the cross in the air.

"You are absolved."

He turns to look at me. His eyes are cloudy and seem to have a hard time focusing.

"I feel a hastiness," he says. "I've got to get ready to go. Time to go."

I wipe the tears away and stand up.

"I'll get your kids."

Mr. Wright closes his eyes and falls into a deep sleep. His breathing is shallow and abrupt, like that of the woman Dorothy in her final hours.

"Thank you for being my friend, Charlie." ൞

CHARLIE

THE WRITER BOY IS talking, but someone has turned the volume down. I can feel his sadness radiate, but I can do nothing and he keeps fading. Everything's disintegrating. He and I both know I will die soon, whatever that means. His face, so fresh and unlined, shimmers like a mosaic of blue raindrops. He forces a smile toward me, but a breeze sweeps it away and replaces him with the swing set my Uncle Joe built when I was seven. All splinters and squeaky links of cold chain. I scrunch my feet together and lean into it. Again. Higher. More. My hands slip free of the metal and my tiny body hurtles through the air. Bare feet slide to a stop in cool sand.

Was this the seed from whence the flying dreams grew? It's all so abstract, the lessons for learning to fly. No, not flying, more like swimming when it comes down to it. The wide spot in Barley Creek. I hold my breath and push cupped hands through the water. Hazy silence. My fingers reach out and read the pebbles lining the muddy bottom. I'm an eel, a merman wiggling through the green, earthy wetness. At home Ma is cranking homemade vanilla ice cream. Dad's turn comes when her arm tires, then I'm on deck. Later we'll squat on the back porch, listen to the growl of summer cicadas, and drift.

In my dreams I can only fly as high as the treetops. Once when the kids were little, Mike the youngest talked me into buying a cockatiel. Mike's doe eyes studied every motion as I gingerly trimmed the bird's feathers just enough to keep it from flying far. We grew used to the hobbled lime–colored bird flitting about the house, leaking shit everywhere in its path. But the wings grew quickly and the kids were careless. I was careless. The cockatiel slipped past the open door and flew into a nearby tree. While the kids snoozed, I chased that damn crap machine from tree to tree. Its wings still weren't grown–in enough for a longer hop. I rose on tippy toe and swatted at it. The bird flew up one branch higher and waited me out. Thus the dance between us began. One tree, then another, then back. About dawn, it landed on my shoulder, looked at me with innocent, bloodshot eyes, opened its little beak and laughed.

I wanted to be a Martian. My folks were earthlings; I was something more. Tin foil antennae sprouted from my noggin and a weird language of clicks and hiccups communicated my strangeness to Mom and Dad. First, there's liftoff. Imagine my body is a helium–filled balloon. Use the hands. Gently at first. Flap. Push down as feet drift upward. It gets easier soon. Think happy thoughts, stay in the moment or crash.

Sometimes it's hard to stay up there. Strangers grasp at my feet, strain to pull me to ground. In slumber, the authorities are always mistakenly out to nab me for murder, when all I've ever destroyed are a pesky cockroach or four, one marriage or three, and countless rusty dreams.

Flying is better than the best sex, more freeing that the tablet of acid I took with two of Mike's jock pals while still in full–on grief after his death. Strange visions that night! The boys played thundering rap music while I nodded and pretended to relate. Frankly, the stuff was angry noise. Give me Sinatra belting out, "That's Life." But that day I couldn't escape the rap beat that filled the room, pressed down like a giant thumb on my skull, wrapped meaty fingers around my throat. I lifted the window and thrust my face out into the night, greedily sucking in cool air. Down below, laughing college girls were covering the trees with toilet paper. The streamers curled into words. HA HA HO HO HEE HEE. I leaned out for a closer look and tumbled two stories into a bush. Slow motion all the way down. It was like I understood the meaning of life, and the truth was one big joke. I couldn't stop laughing. But in the morning, no matter how much I strained my poor old brain, I couldn't remember life's big secret. That door had shut tight. As the kids say, bad trip.

Another dream: hovering above Barley Creek I could almost fathom life's mysteries again. The creek ran along a fault line. One side rose up as a rocky cliff. Standing on the edge was Janice. Mike's Janice. My Janice. Her makeup was heavier than in real life, and her dress was one of those blousy Mexican numbers that were all the rage back in the sixties when I was on the tail end of being young. She raised her index finger and pointed at me.

"Hi," she said.

"Hi," I replied.

As soon as I uttered the word, my body began to sink toward the ground.

I was shacking up with another dame by then, someone closer to my age range and mildly to partly boring. I awoke in the morning to the metallic squeal of the modern day telephone. I answered with a half–asleep, "Yes?"

"Hi," the caller replied. It was Janice calling to catch up.

"Hi," I said.

Bob is crying by my bedside. It's the worst for him. If only we could have communicated, ever. When my old man died, one of his running buddies told me the old tripe that you don't become a man until your father dies. Ready or not. I mouth the words "I'm sorry" to Bob, but still no sound. My dreams and waking life have been poured into a stew pot and stirred into a fiery mess I hardly recognize but for a few floating lumps. Sinatra? "Start spreading the news. I'm leaving today." Taking flight. It all went by so quickly.

Snapshots. My first love (Sorry, kids, it's not your mother!) with her cheek pressed to the dusty wooden floor smiling at a fat, formerly stray cat as it slept. We were broke, the ceiling was stained from the latest leaks and both were beautiful, the woman and the feline curled at my feet. Driving a hundred miles an hour down Kill Hill, my best friend Scott Fenway screaming. Me grinning and tempting death. "Luck be a lady tonight." The steamboat's throaty wail as it sluiced along the mighty Mississippi. The sad void in my daughter Carla's eyes one week after my baby boy's funeral when she caught me kissing his girlfriend Janice.

My only daughter strokes my hand and whispers in my ear. I'm so sorry, little girl. Forgive your old man. I never meant to send you to the psychiatrist's couch. No parent ever means harm. I tried to build a strong foundation for you all. But in the end I was just another Daedalus. You know, he was an architect like me. He built the wings so he and his kid could escape harm, but his boy Icarus didn't listen to Daedalus' warnings and flew too close to the sun. Listen to me, kids. Let it go. Make your own mistakes. Like Sinatra, I did it my own flawed way; you do it yours. Quick. Time is running out. It's the last dance. The final curtain. Reincarnate me as a bird, boys. I'm ready to soar.

How's it go again? First, there's liftoff. Imagine my body is a helium–filled balloon. Use the hands. Gently at first. Flap. Push down as feet drift upward. Higher. Drift with the wind. At the treetops, grab a handful of leaves and bark. Hang on and sway in the breeze until it's time to let go. How do I know when to let go and fly toward the sun? I'm waiting for the signal. ☙

THE LEAP

MR. WRIGHT'S KIDS FILE down the hall to see him. I watch their plodding steps as they inch along, as if they are the condemned, not their dad. Carla reaches out and lays her palm on Bob's shoulder. I don't know what I've learned about death. It's as scary and inescapable as ever, but I do know I'll miss Charlie Wright, and I envy his kids.

The hospice is too quiet now. The nurses are taking care of business. The residents are silent in their beds. No screams just yet. I imagine their eyes counting the holes in the ceiling tiles, counting the seconds left. I wander to the visitor side and find one woman sprawled across a couch, her face hidden beneath a mystery novel. The title is *Dreadful Selfish Crime*. The television is on, but the sound is turned off. A woman on screen holds up a bottle of household cleaner. For the spotless house, free of all unwanted trouble and fear. Her eyes are glassy, her teeth a nuclear white. An alien in the hospice's world of raw, in–your–face truth.

I push open the door, walk across the commemorative bricks and into the parking lot. The air is cool and damp. The soft echo of children playing mixes with the rhythmic trill of hidden crickets. Playing games until the last ounce of light is squeezed from the sun is what it means to be young and clean. When did making up my own story become so impossible? When did I start feeling old and stale? Charlie Wright is more than double my age, but I wouldn't have known it until today. It's time for me to grow young again. I spot an empty soda can by the curb and race toward it, digging my shoe in. The can bounces down the street and stops.

I smile, but it takes the last bit of energy in my body. My legs are rubbery as I go back into the honesty of the hospice. I curl up on the couch by the nurse's station and close my eyes. My body is a stone in a rushing stream. Yes, I've found my story; it's been within me all along. But the weight of this place has a hold of my soul as I drift into blurry dreams.

∽ ∽ ∽

Sarah and I and two of her friends from high school are in my father's house surrounded by rustic wooden bookshelves. We're drinking beer, pulling books out at random and tossing them about the room. The books bubble and burst as the carpet reaches up to envelope them. I look over by the kitchen and spot my father, only he's younger, maybe thirty, with wavy hair and a deep tan. Something about his movement is not quite right. Then I realize, of course, he's dead.

"How's it going?" I say.

He nods.

Sarah frowns at me.

I point.

"It's Dad."

He fractures and fades.

Suddenly I'm back in college, but it's now. I hadn't actually finished one course and the officials have caught up with me. Back then I slept in every day, and now I realize it's a month into the class and I've done it again.

I race down the hall, bumping into hollow–eyed students. When I slide into the room, the professor passes me a test. I grab it and sit.

The instructions say: "Build it." On the desk is a large mound of brown clay. It's cool and airy to the touch. I dig my fingers in and stretch the clay across the room. It expands into a rainbow of colors and swallows desks, students, half–full soda cans. The teacher does the backstroke over to me.

"Not bad," he says. "But you'd better get the door for the old man."

I jolt upright and look around. The nurse's station is deserted, the patient wing dark and silent. The copy machine across from me whirs to life. I reach in and pull out a photocopy of someone's face smashed against the glass. Is it my own?

The door to the patio is open. I peer out. Mr. Wright's cloud of white hair disappears around the corner, and I follow stepping stones that get farther and farther apart. My cartoon legs streeeeeeeetch across and I pick up the pace. I can just make out the heel of his shoe as he turns into a store.

"When is a boy, not a boy?" a distant voice drawls. "Why, when he turns into a store." *Groan*. "You've heard that one, buddy boy?"

The grass around me sprouts higher and higher. I swim through until I reach a gate with a sign: EXACT CHANGE ONLY.

I push through and spy Mr. Wright stepping onto a dock. He moves to the end of a twisting line of perhaps a hundred people, maybe more. I rush to him, but a bony man wearing red suspenders gets there first.

"No pushing, bub!"

Mr. Wright turns and waves the man past him.

"Come to see me off?" He winks. "Good call."

"Where are we?" I ask.

"Waiting for my ship to come in. Ought to be any minute."

As he speaks, Mr. Wright's snow white hair turns salt and pepper gray.

A man wearing a flat straw hat and a pink bow tie strolls along the line.

"Anyone here know the meaning of life?"

I recognize his drawl from before. The man reaches down, picks up a banjo and begins to strum.

"Pipe up, folks. Don't be shy. Hum a few bars and I'll pick it up lickety–split."

Mr. Wright puts his arm around my shoulder and grins.

"I remember him," he says. "A complete and total ham. My mother didn't cotton much to this last time. Too cornpone. Say, did you notice I've got two legs to stand on again? Heaven."

The banjo player stops in front of me, tips his hat, and stares with wide eyes.

"Know the difference between death and an electric eel? People aren't afraid to talk about electric eels! *Shocked* you with that one, didn't I?"

I cover my eyes. The steamship's deep–throated whistle announces its arrival. I look up, and it stretches across the water in front of me in glowing white.

"Tough crowd," the banjo player says. "You folks look like a naughty nautical bunch. Except for this fellow." He points at me. "Do you have a ticket to ride, buddy, old pal o' mine?"

I shake my head.

"You look a bit sheepish. Sheep should be neither seen nor herd. Herd. Get it?"

"I thought cattle were in herds," I say.

He pushes me back as the gangplank is lowered and people begin to file aboard the ship. They all clutch small bundles. I look at Mr.

Wright. His hair is a deep brown, his face unlined and he also carries a bundle.

"Wood to stoke the fire," Mr. Wright says. "A long journey ahead."

He reaches through the crowd and rests his hand on mine.

"What now?" I say.

"For you, life. Go explore. Make some messes."

"And you?"

"Don't you just love a great mystery?"

He giggles like a young boy and leaps onto the boat.

I move to follow, but the banjo player blocks my path and begins to strum again.

"You know the difference between the dead and the living?"

"Yeah," I say.

"Good answer."

ೞ ೞ ೞ

A hand shakes me awake. I stand and see the tears in Carla's eyes. She starts to speak, then puts her palm over mine and hands me something. It's the pocket angel I gave her father.

"He doesn't need protection any more," she says.

"You do," I say. "Keep it."

I reach over and place the chain around her neck.

"Thanks."

The grief and the tears combine and seem to burst forth from her pores. She puts her hand over her mouth and turns back toward Mr. Wright's former room. I look over and see the door to the smoking area is open.

I shut it, but I don't follow Carla. I know for certain that I will never again set foot in one of the patient rooms here. The hospice is almost done with me, and I am full to the brim with it.

Instead I go to the volunteer office and turn on the computer. I type quickly, adrenaline shooting from my fingertips. Not a screenplay. Something else today. The screenplay will come.

The printer spits out my words, and I go back to the hallway by the computer. It is quiet, but I can see motion by Charlie's former room. I pull down the evacuation plan sign and insert my page in the frame. When it's in place, I stand back and admire my handiwork.

EVACUATION PLAN

1. IT IS ESSENTIAL that the human form leave through the back door so as to provide the least possible intrusion to the life of the hospice. This action takes into account the needs of families, staff, and other future travelers.
2. MEN (ONE YOUNG, one old) in blue suits and sporting fresh haircuts will arrive as if by magic shortly after cessation of breath. Do not be alarmed by the plastic wristbands they carry. These are essential to their service. These men (sometimes women) seldom smile, but tend to be of an even disposition and are always polite. Never date them.
3. SPIRITS ARE DIRECTED to the exit next to the copy machine. This door will remain slightly ajar to guide the journey. This is also our designated smoking area. Please resist the urge to slam this door upon departure. While this provides a dramatic effect, it can alarm the uninitiated.
4. YOU MAY NOTICE nurses ducking into back rooms to cry in private at your passing. This is normal. They like you. They are professionals. They say (mostly) nice things behind your back. Nurses brought you pain meds, remember? Consider them your travel agents and proceed toward your exit gate.
5. IMMEDIATE DEPARTURE IS not required. Feel free to linger and collect your thoughts. Stop in the lobby and peruse a book or magazine. Curl up in the fresh roses and breathe deeply. If you are lucky enough to die on a day when musicians are present, float freely among the harp strings and sway with the flute's notes. Yodel. Hum. Dancing is not out of the question.
6. HAUNTING IS STRICTLY forbidden unless prior consent in granted. Please be kind to our resident ghosts by respecting their space. After all, they respected yours during your stay at the hospice. Remember the kind hands rubbing your feet? The gentle smile hovering over your bed?
7. FAMILY WILL LEAVE the facility in their own time; do not attempt to join them. This will only lead to trouble for all involved. You are on a new journey now. Consider instructing relatives to stop

by and touch the hands in the sculpture near the hospice entrance. You and I know these are REAL hands. Give them a shake. High five. Low five. Five on the side. Thumbs up. V for victory. Peace out, sister. A friendly touch is not to be taken lightly.

8. AS A KINDNESS to your kin, work with them prior to your departure to select a memorial message to be placed on a brick in the rear patio. "Good luck" is not sufficient, and "We'll miss you" is a bit obvious. "We love you, Doodle Bug" is better. "A bluebonnet in God's halo" is heavenly. Seek the unique. After all, you only lived once. "Buena Suerte, Lil Bro." Now you're getting the hang of it!
9. FROLIC. PLAY. LIGHT a candle. Throw a smooth stone in the river. Look ahead, not backward, my friend. Leave your luggage behind. Just think: no more bedpans!
10. WHEN ALL ELSE is in doubt, leap.

The End

A DALTON READERS' GUIDE TO

EVACUATION PLAN

ઌ ઌ ઌ

Joe M. O'Connell

A CONVERSATION WITH JOE M. O'CONNELL

Your background includes years as a journalist. How did that affect the way you approached this book?

Perhaps it prepared me to ask the difficult questions. This novel grew out of time I spent with terminally ill people at Hospice Austin's Christopher House. I had the opportunity to go in and talk to the dying and listen to their stories. The book combines my skills as a nonfiction writer and fiction writer. Interestingly, I took copious notes while at Christopher House, but I never once looked at them when writing the book. I was intent on it being a work of fiction, not a recounting of my personal experiences.

Some readers might question Matt's motives for going to the hospice. What would you say to them?

I'd say their instincts are good. In the end Matt is deceiving himself about why he is in the hospice. He's essentially an artist looking for a subject, when that subject has all along been himself. This to me is a statement about being a writer. He's a collector of stories.

The subtitle of the book is "a novel from the hospice," yet it could be confused for a book of short stories. Can you explain why you see it as a novel?

I've gotten this reaction even from other writers, but to me it would be like calling a chocolate chip cookie a collection of chips. That discounts the cookie that holds it all together. Each story is a chip, but none are worth eating (if you'll excuse me extending the metaphor) without the dough that gives it all cohesive meaning. The form was inspired greatly for me by reading two books by two wonderful writers: *A Feast of Love* by Charles Baxter and *July, July* by Tim O'Brien, but the device dates back to the beginnings of the European novel. Am I the only one getting hungry for a cookie?

Many of the stories involve fathers and sons. What are we to make of this?

Well, we also have fathers and daughters. But the core of this book is the personal story of loss that Matt eventually reveals to Charlie

Wright. I wrote the skeleton that became Matt's story as a way of dealing with the death of my own father when I was in my late twenties. The details of death there are real, but the story and the characters aren't. My father was also an architect, but Mr. Wright is not based on him. If anything that character's got a little of Frank Lloyd Wright, a brilliant man who thought a lot about family but was by most accounts a poor father. I'm a new parent and read a quote recently from the comedian Jerry Seinfeld about how our kids are there to replace us and perhaps that's it. But also, I believe to truly become adults we've got to forgive our parents for being human and realize we have to take responsibility for our own happiness.

You're a columnist writing about the film industry for The Austin Chronicle *and* Dallas Morning News. *Is that why you chose to make Matt a screenwriter? Any filmmakers influence you?*

When I received a residency that allowed me to complete this book—thanks to the writer Dao Strom who worked with me during that time—I was also preparing to teach a college screenwriting class. I subscribe to the black hole theory of writing: When in the zone, anything I come in contact with may be sucked into the work. Some have said the narrative reminds them of my fellow Texan Richard Linklater, particularly his films *Slacker* and *Waking Life* for their episodic nature. I've interviewed Linklater, but don't know him personally. Perhaps it more shows we're about the same age and have similar obsessions with subjects like dreams and the creation of reality.

What do you want readers to learn about hospice care from the novel?

That hospice is about life more than it's about death. One book club showed early interest in reading my book, but also concern that it would be depressing. That's the problem hospice has. Unless you've been in the environment, then you probably don't realize how much joy is to be found there. Hospice—whether home care or residential as portrayed in my novel—is about empowering people to leave this world on their own terms and to be able to say a proper goodbye. I'm passionate about using this novel to provoke discussion about hospice care. That's important.

Can you recommend any other books for people wishing to explore the subject of death and dying? Other books that influenced you in general?

Sure. Death is a subject we need to quit shying away from and discuss openly. These first two works get at the heart of it, and the others also dig deep into the human condition:

- *The Year of Magical Thinking* by Joan Didion
- *How We Die: Reflections on Life's Final Chapter* by Sherwin B. Nuland, M.D.
- *Meditations from a Movable Chair* by Andre Dubus
- *One Day in the Life of Ivan Denisovich* by Aleksandr Solzhenitsyn
- *Man's Search for Meaning* by Viktor Frankl

QUESTIONS FOR DISCUSSION

1. IS MATT A likable character? How does his role as an observer at the hospice color what you think of him? Does that perception change?
2. WHAT DO YOU think "The Guy in the Hall" gets from his run-ins with himself? Is he sane?
3. WHAT SURPRISES YOU about Matt and Charlie Wright as characters?
4. WE LEARN THE stories of two hospice nurses. How are the circumstances that brought them to the profession different? The same?
5. MATT ORIGINALLY SEES Charlie Wright's family as being perfect. How does his view of them change? What does this say about families and death?
6. A CHARACTER IN the story of "The Student" talks about God and his inability to help them. What do you make of this? Is this echoed elsewhere in the novel? What role does religion play for characters in the novel?
7. "THE MORTICIAN" SUFFERS loss after almost wishing for it. How do you feel about this character's mixed emotions?
8. WHAT ROLE DOES the hospice as a place play in the story? How does this agree/disagree with your expectations?
9. WHAT SECRETS ARE being kept by the characters? What effects do these have on their relationships?
10. THE BOOK CONTAINS a couple of stories of childhood. How does what characters were as children stay with them later in life? Can we ever escape our past?
11. MATT SAYS THE boy on the bicycle will spend the rest of his life learning to forgive his father. What do you make of this?
12. MR. WRIGHT DOESN'T seem to know what awaits him in death. Does this trouble him? Does it trouble you as a reader?

ABOUT THE AUTHOR

Photo by Caroline Ulbrich

Joe O'Connell has met a mass murderer, prowled a crack house, and spat seeds at a watermelon thump. He's a Texas native whose early career focused on small-town journalism. He earned an MFA in creative writing from Southwest Texas State University where he worked long distance with the late short story master Andre Dubus. O'Connell's stories have appeared in *The G.W. Review*, *Other Voice*, *Confrontation*, *Lullwater Review*, and many other journals. His stories have taken first prize at both the Deep South Writers Conference and the Louzelle Rose Barclay Awards. Of late, he teaches writing to graduate students at St. Edward's University and to undergraduates at Austin Community College. He turned a budding career as a movie extra—otherwise known as "scenery"—into a gig as a film industry columnist for the *Dallas Morning News* and *The Austin Chronicle* and previously for the *Austin American-Statesman*. He also has contributed to *Variety* and *Texas Monthly*. Joe lives outside Austin with his wife and newborn son. ***www.joemoconnell.com***

∽ ∽ ∽

O'Connell hopes to work with hospice organizations in outreach efforts in one of two ways:

1. FOR REIMBURSEMENT OF travel expenses only, he will come and read from the book at your group's event. Or, he will help hospice groups recruit local actors to read from the book as part of a performance reading.
2. DALTON PUBLISHING HAS agreed to offer the book (cover price: $13.95) to hospice groups for $9.00 a copy (plus shipping) for sale at events at full price—with the difference going directly to the hospice organization. The publisher and author will aid efforts to get local media attention for hospice events related to the book.

∽ ∽ ∽

O'Connell also will speak—either by telephone or in person if possible—to any book clubs choosing to read the book. He can be contatcted at: ***therealjoeo@gmail.com***.